THE DARK WAY

Stories from the Spirit World

TOLD BY

VIRGINIA HAMILTON

ILLUSTRATED BY

LAMBERT DAVIS

Harcourt Brace Jovanovich, Publishers

SAN DIEGO   NEW YORK   LONDON

HBJ

Text copyright © 1990 by Virginia Hamilton
Illustrations copyright © 1990 by Lambert Davis

Permissions acknowledgments appear on page 155,
which constitutes a continuation of the copyright page.

Library of Congress Cataloging-in-Publication Data
Hamilton, Virginia.
The dark way: stories from the spirit world/told by
Virginia Hamilton; illustrated by Lambert Davis.
p.   cm.
Summary: A collection of folktales, legends, and myths
involving the supernatural, from cultures around the world.
ISBN 0-15-222340-1
ISBN 0-15-222341-X (ltd. ed.)
1. Tales [1. Supernatural—Folklore. 2. Folklore.]
I. Davis, Lambert, ill. II. Title.
PZ8.1.H154Dar   1990
398.2—dc20   90-36251

Printed in the United States of America
First edition
A B C D E

To the Timeless Traveler: the unquenchable spirit of us all.

—V. H.

To children around the world and their limitless imaginations.

—L. D.

CONTENTS

Dark is a way and light is a place . . .
—DYLAN THOMAS

Between then and now is the channel where misty hoarfrost rises to the darkening shadows. And melting ice needles dribble down like glistening drool from a monster's fangs. Between thought and unthinking is this course of the shapeshifter, shrouded in gloom. Whether it be monster, gorgon, trickster, ghost, imp, fairy, elf, devil, phantom, or witch — all of these twitch, they change, nightmaring, slumbering there. In the Dark Way.

The Way is beyond us, yet near — where unearthly spirits wait. Some will be friendly to us and helpful, and some will not. Others will take on frightful forms, even comical, human and animal or godlike. But once awakened, all are eager to leap into our existence, into the corners of our imaginations, into our fearful or caring thoughts.

They creep into our homes, into the kindling box by the fire; they float into our closets, cellars, and glide onto our paths. Wherever there is room for them, they can come crawling, growing. Whenever the light is soft or dimmed or has gone out, they come. Their presence charges the space around us. Someone of us is made aware of one of them by sensing the eerie "otherness" of its nature.

All at once, you know you are not alone. Out from the Dark Way streams deathless power. You glimpse its aura; you feel its unnatural energy in a touch.

Take care, then. The presence may be with you, whether you recognize it or not, whether you believe in it or not. Hope for the kindness of fairy; beware of devilish witchery, trickery.

As long as we are here, the un-human will be there between was and is, in the gloom of the Dark Way. Between awake and asleep, midst being and not being, it strives, it vies, for us. So it has been for ages, and surely always will be.

Chew on the above with one ounce of rue and a grain of salt!

Tales out of darkness are frightful fun and have satisfied an ancient need in humans to make order out of disorder and to control their environment. Since the time of the first community, humans have set moral boundaries beyond which they travel at their peril.

The twenty-five stories in *The Dark Way: Stories from the Spirit World* have limitations imposed by a commonality of rules for right conduct. The unruliness of human emotions is bounded by fear and retribution—what will happen to me if I do what I want and not what they say is allowed? What might be my punishment? I want to climb that sacred mountain, but what will happen if I do? I want to go here, not there. What will they do to me if I stay by the fire, alone, and do not go with all of them? They say something unseen will come and get me—will it? I fear that if I do wrong, the spirit of the wind will carry me off, and I will not be seen again. . . .

In the story "Fenris, the Wolf," the gods make ever stronger chains to contain the wolf child grown into a ferocious monster. The moral is clear: control—bind—the animal passions within us.

"Joseph Golem" describes a being made of clay that those who are persecuted create and bring to life to protect them from their persecutors.

Other tales express fears of death. In "The Banshee," a screaming fairy ghost is a fatal warning for the one who hears it. In "Rolling Rio, the Gray Man, and Death," the fisherman actually wrestles Death and comes out the winner. The outcome is similar in "Yama, the God of Death," in which the god of the underworld is undone by his son, who threatens to tell Yama's whereabouts to his arguing wife.

Quite naturally, we fear and regret that our lives must end. We create stories that make us larger than life and better than human. Our desire for immortality is expressed in such tales as "Everlasting Life," the story of a maiden who from a dream gains life without end. In "Medusa," the lovely girl of the title is mortal but is changed into an immortal gorgon by the jealous goddess, Athena.

Other stories in *The Dark Way* are humorous, depicting spirited trickster characters. In "Tanuki Magic Teakettle," an animal transforms itself into a teakettle and gains fame and fortune. Bouki and Malice in "The Free Spirits, Bouki and Malice," are talking animal tricksters, one of whom is stupid (Bouki), and the other (Malice) is clever. It is Malice who usually gets himself and Bouki into and then out of trouble.

The Dark Way, then, provides us with all manner of stories in which the frailty of human beings in all their fear and trembling is outlined against the light — the greatness of earth and the heavens. Undoubtedly these stories may frighten you. They may make you smile and laugh as well. But above all, they will deeply entertain you in your most secret, fearful heart.

VIRGINIA HAMILTON

THE DARK WAY

The Banshee

Some have seen it and wished they hadn't. The Banshee. Have you heard tell of it? Go down by the river, they say. And there you will find the Banshee smacking the water with its hands.

Be on the road between woods and nothing, and home at the dark of the moon, and you might see it, that is, if someone is to die. For the Banshee cries for Death. Truly, it be Death's announcer.

Some have seen it at the crossroads when there is but a sliver of moon to light the carriage. Look out! There it stands in the middle of the road. It is a long, thin figure of a woman, don't you know. And, oh, how she can wail! No woman ever sounded so dreadful, so pitiful, and so inhuman!

Some say the Banshee is a fairy. Maybe it was once. But now *she* is tall and silent. She looks deadly with her head uncovered. Her long white hair flows loosely down her shoulders. Her face is forlorn and twisted in agony. Her hand points to the grand house next, down the road. And with the other arm pushing and waving, she directs us to go to that place.

The Banshee claps her hands loudly for long minutes and wraps the cloak tightly around her, like a shroud. Then she gives out with that awful wail. It is called "the scream of the Banshee." It is like no other. Pray that you never hear it!

Some say they have been awakened by the Banshee's scream and lived to tell the tale. The wail of the Banshee would come at quick intervals. The sound of it is not like a voice, not like an instrument. It is more devilish than either and more terrifying than any music.

She is invisible to some. But others awakened by her scream believe she is a woman, a ghost or a fairy. Still others who see her say she is a snake woman, that long ago she was punished for wrongdoing.

The Banshee is known to sit wailing under a tree that has been struck by lightning. Some have seen her at the river washing blood from the clothing of those who will die after they have heard her voice.

Heard tell that an enormous black coach and four horses announce the coming of the Banshee. This coach-and-four holds a coffin and is drawn by headless horses and driven by a headless man. If that coach goes rattling by, do not run to open its door to see inside. For if you do, a basin of blood will be thrown in your face!

There! Look closely! But look only once. Down to her navel the Banshee is a woman. But below her waist, she is a scaly serpent and must be cursed as such.

Cover your ears at the first wail of the Banshee. It is said that they who hear her screams at dawn will drop dead by nightfall.

I have given you fair warning!

COMMENT

Banshee comes from the Irish *bean* (ban), "a woman," and *sídhe* (shee), "a fairy," and the Scottish Gaelic *Ban Sith*. Hence, the Banshee means "woman of the fairies." In Irish folklore the Banshee is a female ghost or fairy who gives notice of the coming death of a family member by clapping her hands and letting loose with bloodcurdling shrieks. She is described variously as a snake woman, a beautiful maiden, or an old woman with long white hair, dressed in a cloak or a death shroud. Originally, the Banshee was a spirit attached to highborn families. And there are many family stories of Banshees. But mainly she is talked and told about as a warning to those who may innocently cross her path. The phrase "scream like a Banshee" is quite common even today.

Rolling Rio, the Gray Man, and Death

He was a fisherman, was Rolling Rio. He was a big, well-built man with the power of ten his own size.

One fine day, he was ready to go fishing, and he asked his best friend to go with him.

"I don't like the feel of the air," said the friend.

"But you know how to row better than two men," said Rolling Rio. "You handle the oars, and I'll cast the nets and take care of the firepot and frying the fish we catch."

"Don't think so," said his friend. "The weather is looking like it is about to fall down on us. You'd better take care, Rio."

"Well, good-bye then," said Rio. "I don't mind going it alone when I have to." So Rolling Rio went off by himself in his eight-seat boat. He rowed to a place he knew where he had good luck with his nets. But this day, no fish would have him.

"There must be fish out here," he thought. "When my boat is full and set so low that the sea tries to fill it up, I'll go home!"

He went to another good place he knew, but he came up empty again, as though his nets had holes in them. "I swear I'll not go home until my boat is full!" he told himself. He rowed on, casting his nets here and there along his way. But he caught not one fish. Rolling Rio went so far that the near shore appeared odd to him. He knew his seascape and shoreline as well as anyone. For that reason, he did not turn back. He cast his nets all around, but he took no fish at any casting.

"Strange," he thought. "I know there are fish. Nothing can empty the sea unless it's me, Rolling Rio!"

Evening came, and the sea seemed to darken as did the sky. Waves were heavy and bouncy. Rio was swept along swiftly. When night fell, he was hungry and blue and tired of fishing empty. By the time he decided to make for shore, he was drenched clear through and cold with the shivers.

He brought the boat in easily enough. But the beach had no size at all. Just a fringe of palmettos, driftwood and seaweed, and rotten pieces of broken ships beached long ago. All was quiet, save for the sea breaking over the sand, and the wind rising in a mournful wail in his ears.

"I've been all over these waters and shores," Rio whispered to himself, "but this place I fail to remember. I don't know it, and I don't like it."

He gathered bleached driftwood and made a fire. Soon he was warming, and he sat awhile, just letting the heat enter him, making him a strong man again. But the fire wouldn't stay, even though the wood was dry as could be. It had warmed him, and now it quickly cooled him. It made only a low, steady flame with a long gray wisp of smoke that rose in a trembling stream.

Rio kept a firepot on the boat when he traveled the sea. He took a red-hot coal from it and put it in the fire under fresh driftwood. He leaned near to blow on the coal. And then Rolling Rio froze.

A long, bony foot was there, right in the fire. It had long, skinny toes, and smoke seemed to come from under the toenails.

Rio carefully looked up. There stood a gray man towering above him in the dark. Just one foot was stuck in Rio's fire; the other was somewhere outside the ring of firelight. The gray man was two stories tall. He was covered with gray ashes, but underneath he was black as soot. He scowled down at Rio with smoky, dark eyes.

"Who asked you onto my beach?" rumbled the gray man.

"Well, if it's yours, you can have it. I'm leaving," said Rolling Rio. He took up all his gear, his firepot, his nets — all that he'd taken out of his boat — and he put it back. Then, swiftly, Rio shoved off; he took hold of his oars and pulled as hard as he could away from shore.

Now the wind was high and mighty, blowing gale hard. Rio's boat acted up. She wouldn't head up her bow. She stayed too low, and incoming waves nearly swamped her. Her stern, too, was down when it oughtn't to have been.

Rio thought to move his gear forward, hoping to balance things better. He turned, reaching behind him, and saw he wasn't alone. No, indeed!

There sat the awful, gigantic gray man who had caused him to leave the beach. His big, bony feet were wrapped in Rio's nets. His huge black self was about to sink the boat.

Rolling Rio took to rowing like he never had before. A great gale now was blowing. The boat lifted high on waves as tall as hills. The gray man never moved himself in any way. Through the growing storm, great swells of water washed over the boat and filled the bottom.

"You better had take my gourd and bail!" Rio shouted through the din. But the gray man did not lift a finger to help.

Rio rowed and rowed. His arms ached, they were so tired. But he was Rolling Rio. He wasn't afraid. Waves smashed at the boat, once nearly turning her under.

It thundered and it lightninged. "Oh, look at that! Hear that?" cried Rio to the gray man. The gray man said not a word.

"It's almost like you're not there!" shouted Rio later, over the moaning, crying storm. But the gray man said nothing.

Rio could barely steer; there was such a thunder of weather and waves. The very sea seemed to cry out as it swelled ever higher.

Rio's hands stung him, and looking down, he saw that he had rubbed the skin off, and his palms were raw and bloody.

He spoke again, urgently, to the gray man. "Friend, take those oars and pull your share. I am giving out."

The gray man scowled. "If she turns bottoms up, you'll drown," he said to Rolling Rio.

"So will you!" Rio shot right back.

"Are you afraid to die?" asked the gray man.

"No, not on your life!" Rio replied.

He went on rowing until his hands bled freely, and the oars were slippery and red. There was no sight of land anywhere. "It's time you

helped me!" Rio shouted at the gray man, for he knew he was about to drown.

The gray man said nothing.

Rio said, "So be it, do-nothing man, you and I will go together."

The gray man eyed Rio and nodded. He fell asleep, snoring like the wind.

Rolling Rio rowed on until his eyes were blinded by the salt sea, and blood from his hands settled in the water around his feet. Slowly great Rio lost his strength. He was not afraid, but he could no longer move the oars.

The gray man did nothing to help and said nothing that was a comfort.

Suddenly, Rio's eight-seat boat rose high on a mountain of sea.

"Do something!" Rio shouted to the gray man. "I cannot help us now!"

Sleepily the gray man got up and stood there, pine-top high. He reached with his enormous hands and took Rio's boat by her hull and lifted her, Rio, and himself right out of the water. It happened so fast it made Rio dizzy. They were out of the sea and in the air, moving like the wind. The gray man dropped the boat as lightly as a feather drifting down into the sea. Then he was gone as though he never ever was, never could have been, and never would be.

When Rolling Rio woke up, he was in his boat, and the sun was shining. His nets were full of fish. He had his strength, he wasn't cold and miserable, and not one of his muscles was stiff. His hands had healed overnight, and truly he was great Rio as he had been before.

When he got home, his was the best haul he'd ever made, and he got the most money for it. The whole town said how Rolling Rio went fishing in a gale and had come back full.

That evening Rio stood on the wharf by his boat when a stranger came near. He was a tall man who wore shadow clothes, whose face was dark and still as a mask. But it wasn't the gray man.

"Rolling Rio," said the man, "the town may think you great, but I am greater and stronger, too."

Rio smiled. "Then let's see," he said. "Let us wrestle three throws."

Before they started, the dark man said, "Rio, do you know who I am?"

"No, I do not," Rio answered.

"Look into my eyes," said the dark man. He was the one to blink first. "Doesn't matter," he said, "I'll still throw you."

"Then don't talk! Do it!" said Rolling Rio. He did not guess, but this was old Death himself.

Death caught hold and threw Rio hard.

"It's two out of three," said Rio, panting. He lunged, squeezing Death's ribs until they cracked.

Death gave all his strength. "Now I have you!"

But he didn't have Rolling Rio. For Rio took Death over his hip and threw him.

"God!" Death cried out. He moaned and groaned and got up slowly. His ribs were broken.

"Now it is the final fall," Rio said.

But then Death spoke quickly. "Oh, I beg your pardon, but no," he

said. "I've had enough of you, Rolling Rio. Let old age take you under!" With that, Death strode away, holding his ribs together.

Rolling Rio carried on through his long days and years. He feared no gray man nor Death nor anything. That was the kind of big, brave man he was.

But they say that ever after meeting Rolling Rio, old Death has leaned a little, favoring that one side of his. And unlike Rolling Rio, Death has never had a friend.

COMMENT

This is a gripping, yet curious story, told by a number of North Carolina fishermen in the first free generation after slavery. It is an exaggeration or tall tale, as well as a scare tale. Rolling Rio, who is a John Henry, self-made–man type of individual, can be thought of as a legendary figure who at one time probably existed but whose unusualness was the basis for myth-making. Thus, the real Rio and his ability at sea may have become overblown or distorted by time, fancy, misunderstanding, and superstition.

Baba Yaga, the Terrible

There was a beautiful young daughter of a merchant. Her name was Vas-il-isa. Her mother, who was very ill, gave her a doll. "I give you my blessing with this doll," the mother said. "Always keep it close to you, and show it to no one. If you find yourself in trouble, give the doll a bite to eat, and ask her advice. She will tell you what to do."

Soon the mother died, and it was sad, so sad, for Vasilisa without her. Still, the child had the gift of the doll.

The merchant was very lonely, and so he married again. The stepmother and her daughters came to live in the house with Vasilisa and her father. The stepmother was jealous of Vasilisa's beauty and gave her barely enough food to live. Even so, the child grew prettier and plumper. Her stepmother and stepsisters were ever more hateful, and they grew skinnier and uglier.

Now the truth was this: Vasilisa's doll was helping her. Even when the girl had nothing to eat, she made sure the doll had food. In the tiny room where she slept, Vasilisa would whisper, "Doll, show me, tell me what to do."

The doll ate well and gave Vasilisa good advice. When morning came, she had lit the stove for Vasilisa, had brought water into the kitchen. She'd done all of Vasilisa's chores. Vasilisa could go pick flowers and stroll in the shade.

Time passed, and Vasilisa was old enough to become a bride. Young men came to court her. They would not look at the stepsisters. This made the stepmother dislike Vasilisa even more.

"Not until her older sisters are wed will Vasilisa marry," said the stepmother to the young men.

Now the merchant had to go away for many months to take care of his business. The stepmother waited until he had gone, then moved them all to a house at the edge of a deep, dark forest.

In the forest was a clearing, and in the clearing stood a hut. The hut spun around and around on supports that were chicken legs! And in the hut lived the cruel witch, Baba Yaga. She was ten times uglier than the stepmother and the stepsisters. Some called her Baba Yaga Bony Leg because she looked like a skeleton. She had long, sharp teeth, and she was known to steal, cook, and eat her prey — mainly children. When she wasn't hungry, well, then she used a magic club to turn her victims to stone.

No one went near the house of Baba Yaga, not unless they wanted to be eaten as if they were chickens.

The stepmother made excuses for sending Vasilisa into the forest. But Vasilisa always came back safely. The doll showed her the way and kept her away from the house of Baba Yaga.

One night, there were no candles, and Vasilisa was made to find one.

"Baba Yaga will give you light," said one stepsister.

"Go to Baba Yaga's house," commanded another stepsister.

In her room, Vasilisa whispered to her doll, "Baba Yaga will eat me!"

The doll's eyes grew big and round. "Go where they send you," the doll said, "but keep me with you, and nothing awful will happen to you at Baba Yaga's."

Vasilisa hid the doll in her pocket. She went out into the night to walk in the deep, dark forest.

She walked and walked, on and on. Before she knew it, it was dawn. As the sky lightened, a horseman came galloping by. He had a white face and white clothes. He had a white horse and saddle.

Vasilisa continued on. The sun came up, and a second horseman galloped by. He had a scarlet face, wore scarlet clothes, and his horse and saddle were scarlet.

The doll kept Vasilisa from fearing such strange happenings. Vasilisa walked on the whole day and night and the next day. That evening, she came to the clearing where Baba Yaga's hut stood spinning on chicken legs. Such a sight! Surrounding the house was a fence made from human bones. At the top of the bone posts were skulls with stony eyes. Human leg bones made a gate, with a pair of bony hands for bolts. The lock was a jaw with pointed teeth.

So terrified was Vasilisa that she stood frozen. All at once, a horse-man galloped out of nowhere. His face and clothes and his horse and saddle were black. He spurred his horse right up to the bone gate of Baba Yaga's hut. Then, he vanished.

Darkness fell. The eyes in the skulls atop the gateposts grew bright. Vasilisa stared, clutching the doll in her pocket.

An awful noise came from the forest. Trees groaned. Leaves rustled, and branches creaked. Air stirred wildly.

Baba Yaga came riding in a huge mortar, like a bowl. She rowed herself along the ground using a pestle as an oar. In the other hand, she had a broom, and she swept it along, clearing her path and making a wind storm. She stopped at the gate and sniffed and snorted.

"Ugh!" she said. "I smell a Russian. Who's there?"

Trembling, Vasilisa moved two steps forward. "It's only me, Vasil-isa," said the maiden. "My stepsisters sent me here to get a light from you, since we have none."

"Ah, stay and work for me, and I will give you a light," said Baba Yaga. "And if you think of running away, I'll eat you for dinner!"

Baba Yaga shouted to the gates: "Bolts so strong, unlock — gates so strong, open wide!"

The gates opened. Baba Yaga hurried inside. Vasilisa followed her into the house set on chicken legs as the bone gates clattered shut.

"I'm hungry," said Baba Yaga. "Pretty daughter, go see what's in the oven."

Vasilisa took a piece of kindling and lit a candle from the bright skull eyes on the fence posts. Then she brought food from the oven and drink from the cellar.

Baba Yaga ate and drank it all. She grew to giant size, nearly bursting the seams of the house. Her nose was pressed flat against the ceiling. And her feet were wedged in opposite corners.

Vasilisa had only cabbage soup. She sat with her knees up to her chin in a vacant corner. Huge Baba Yaga took up almost all of the space.

Finally Baba Yaga got ready for bed. "You are to clean everything after I leave tomorrow," she told Vasilisa, and she explained all of the chores. Then Baba Yaga went to sleep, snoring mightily the whole night.

Vasilisa cried and cried. "Baba Yaga will eat me if I don't do what she says," she told her doll.

"Never fear," said the doll. "Go to sleep now, and you'll feel better in the morning."

In the morning, Vasilisa awoke and looked outside. She saw the skull eyes grow dim. The white horseman came galloping by. It was day.

Baba Yaga whistled for her mortar and pestle.

All at once, the scarlet horseman rode by. The sun was up. Baba Yaga climbed into her mortar.

Vasilisa trembled to ask Baba Yaga a question. "Please, tell me who the three horsemen are," she said.

"So now you wish to talk to me," said Baba Yaga. She laughed. "The horsemen are my servants: Dawn, Day, and Night." Then she rowed with the pestle and brushed her tracks away with her broom. A dust storm followed her.

Vasilisa was alone with her doll. To her surprise and happiness, the doll had done all of the day's work for her. It had even weeded Baba Yaga's tangled garden.

"You saved my life again," Vasilisa told her.

"All you have to do is make supper," said the doll, and it climbed back into Vasilisa's pocket.

By suppertime, Vasilisa had made a good meal. Toward evening, she set the table. At dusk, the black horseman rode past the bone gates. Darkness fell. Light glowed from the skull eyes.

Baba Yaga came home, riding, rowing, and sweeping as before.

"Have you done all the work?" she asked.

"It is done, see for yourself," said Vasilisa.

"How did you do everything so quickly?" asked Baba Yaga. She was angry that she could not eat the girl.

"My mother's blessings helped me with my chores," said Vasilisa.

"In that case, I want you to leave," said Baba Yaga. "I can't stand humans who are blessed." She shoved Vasilisa out through the gates. And taking a skull with bright eyes, she stuck it on a pole and gave it over to Vasilisa. "A bright light for your stepsisters!" she said, cackling.

Vasilisa ran home all through the night. The skull lit her way. The glowing eyes grew dim only with the dawn. By the time Vasilisa reached home, she was ready to throw the skull away. But it spoke to her.

"Keep me!" it said. "Take me to your stepmother."

At the house, there was no light. The stepmother and the sisters came out. "We haven't been able to keep a flame lit since you've been gone," the stepmother told her. She took the skull inside. Its feverish eyes stared straight at the stepmother and stepsisters. As they moved around, the blazing gaze of the skull followed.

In the morning, Vasilisa woke up to find her stepmother and stepsisters burned to cinders. They lay in piles, all shriveled and black. The skull eyes had set them on fire.

Vasilisa and the doll were alone again together. Vasilisa buried the skull six feet under the ground. She locked the house and went away to town. There she waited for her dear father to return. She found a room in a house with a poor woman. She and her doll spun thread into fine cloth. The poor woman took the cloth to the emperor.

"Ah, make me shirts from this delicate cloth!" he commanded.

Vasilisa and her doll worked hard until the shirts were finished. Then the poor woman took them to the palace. The emperor was pleased and invited the woman to bring her seamstress. When he saw Vasilisa, he fell in love. The emperor asked her to marry him, and Vasilisa said she would.

Everything was strangely quiet when her father came home. He was sad to have lost his wife and stepdaughters.

"If I had been here, they might have been kinder to Vasilisa," he thought. But his heart filled with joy at his daughter's good fortune.

"Ah, Vasilisa," he said, "You are a good daughter." He and the old woman, too, came to live in the castle with his daughter and the emperor.

So it was that Vasilisa lived happily ever after. She kept the doll in her pocket — always.

COMMENT

Baba Yaga tales come from rural Russia and are quite old. The witch is the best-known Russian folk character. *Baba* is "a peasant woman, a grand-mother"; *Yaga* is "a witch woman." Baba Yaga means "Grandmother Witch." She has great power over the forest and the animals who share it with her. Beasts and birds obey her, as do the winds. She controls time in the appearance of Dawn, Day, and Night.

The One-Inch Boy

Once upon a time, an aging man and woman had no children. And so they prayed, "Give us any kind of child. We do not mind what he is! We will be happy even if he is only an inch tall!"

As life would have it, the prayer was granted, and a teeny-tiny boy was born to the couple. His name was Issun-boshi, or The One-Inch Boy. Oh, One-Inch was a clever child. But he grew no bigger than when he was born. Still, when he grew older, he told his mother and father, "I want to seek my fortune in the capital city. I wish to see the world!"

His parents wanted only his happiness. And so they gave One-Inch all the supplies he would need. They didn't forget bowls and chopsticks, tea and rice. They gave him a sword, which was the size of a fine needle.

Issun-boshi started on his journey. He used a wooden rice bowl as a boat and a chopstick for his rudder in crossing streams. When he reached the city, he was taken at once into a nobleman's service. One-

Inch became a useful servant as the companion of the nobleman's daughter. And he lived in the jewel box on her table. One-Inch and the princess played together each day.

One day, they went to the temple nearby, and on the way back a demon stopped them. "I am going to eat you!" the demon threatened the princess in a great, loud voice.

The demon was an oni, the kind that is huge and green all over. It had three eyes and horns on its head. It had three toes on each ugly foot and three fingers on each out-of-shape hand. The oni carried a club covered with sharp spikes. It lunged at the princess, trying to catch her.

But clever and brave Issun-boshi climbed up the demon as though he were climbing a mountain. When the demon opened its mouth to roar, One-Inch pricked its nose with his needle sword and leaped into its mouth. He pricked the demon's tongue, and that hurt! For as One-Inch knew, a demon's tongue is wet and tender. One-Inch flew out of the oni's mouth on its roar of pain. The oni dropped its spiked club and ran in circles.

Issun-boshi hid himself until he was certain the demon would leave. And it was not long before the oni demon vanished in a violent wind.

The princess then came out of hiding and picked up the club the oni had left behind. She knew that demons sometimes carried magic clubs that, when wished upon, gave what was desired. She swung the club, and she cried out, "I wish Issun-boshi to grow tall!"

At once, One-Inch grew, inch-by-inch, each time the princess swung the club. Finally he was as tall and as handsome a youth as any princess might wish.

"I am grateful to you for saving me from the demon," said the princess.

"And I am grateful to you for making me so tall, your royal highness," said the grown-up boy.

The lord nobleman was very pleased when he heard what had happened. And a few years later, he allowed the former One-Inch to advance in his service. Issun-boshi married the beautiful princess, and they lived a long, happy life.

COMMENT

This story from Japan bears a resemblance to the Grimms' tale of little "Thumbling," who, no bigger than a thumb, is born to a childless couple. The demon here is the Japanese devil, the oni, who can be a giant who eats the whole world, or a vampire, a goblin, or an ogre. His spiked club can grant anything that is desired. Onis are easily fooled, thus they often become comic objects and the butts of jokes when they meddle in human affairs — as the oni does in the above story.

Manabozo

They say he was from an unknown time, was Man-a-bozo. He took form on earth as a great white hare with long, long ears. But he was a god, a manitou. His guard and servant was a wolf who lived in the lodge with him.

One sad day, the wolf drowned. And then Manabozo was by himself, and lonely. "I will find the wolf," he said, "and deliver him to the lodge."

He went to the kingfisher bird to find out what he knew about fishes. For Manabozo reasoned that the drowned wolf would have been eaten by a very big fish.

"I will tell you all I know about fishes," said the kingfisher. "But they didn't eat Wolf. More likely, it was the serpents below who gulped Wolf's body." Ever grateful, Manabozo gave the kingfisher a medal of wampum for his help, to wear around his neck. So it came to pass — the wampum is the white spot the kingfisher wears forever on his chest.

But then Manabozo had a mean thought: "The kingfisher may not be friendly to me at all. He may go down under the water and warn the serpents."

Manabozo hurried to catch the kingfisher. They struggled, but the bird was too swift and broke away. However, his feathers got mussed up in the scuffle, and now all such fishers wear ruffled feathers.

Manabozo went out in his canoe to fish on the lake. He had his war club in his boat. When he wasn't paying attention, something jumped in the boat with him. Manabozo didn't see it. It was a little squirrel, but never mind him right now.

Manabozo put his line down and told the king of fishes to bite on his bait. He called again and again—"Mesh-enah-mah-gwai, king of fishes, hold my bait."

Finally the king of fishes below spoke. "He is trouble, that Manabozo. Trout, take hold of his line." So Trout took the line.

Manabozo drew up the line. Trout was heavy, too, so heavy the canoe almost stood straight up out of the water.

Manabozo shouted at Trout to get off his line. Trout did, too. And by this time, the king of fishes was very tired of Manabozo. So the king took hold of the line himself and let himself be pulled up to the surface. Suddenly the huge king of fishes opened his mouth and swallowed Manabozo and his canoe in one giant gulp.

Manabozo and his boat tumbled one over the other all the way down into the great fish's belly. Manabozo had time to figure out what to do. He wasn't going anywhere now. He took his war club from its place in his canoe. And he climbed to the great fish's heart and struck it as though he struck a drum—Boom! Boom! Boom!

The king of fishes grew dizzy. "That dirty Manabozo has made me sick to my stomach," he said.

Manabozo wedged his canoe across the fish's throat so he wouldn't be thrown up somewhere far from shore where he might drown. And he realized now that there was someone else in the boat with him. For up popped the head of that squirrel, who had been pushing and shoving, helping him all along while he wedged the boat.

"Ah," smiled Manabozo. "I compliment, you, A-ji-daumo!"

Then Manabozo beat his war club again against the great fish's heart. At last, the king of fishes died from the blows, and his lifeless body was washed by waves onto the shore.

Manabozo and Ajidaumo waited inside the dead king of fishes. Soon, many gulls landed and began pecking away at the body. It was not long before Manabozo saw sunlight. Then he saw gulls all around, peering into the opening their beaks had made.

"Brothers, make the hole bigger so my friend and I can get out," called Manabozo.

"Why, look," said the gulls. "There is Manabozo inside the belly of a fish!" They worked very hard, and then, in no time, the great hare was freed.

Manabozo was happy, and he did a good thing then. He said to the gulls, "From this day on, you shall be known as Noble Scratchers because of your kindness to me."

Well, Manabozo never did find Wolf, his old friend, although he went fishing many times.

But the gulls still are Noble Scratchers from that time of the great hare, Manabozo, until tomorrow.

COMMENT

This legendary tale of Manabozo is similar to the Jonah and the whale story from the Holy Bible. It has three pourquoi sections—why the kingfisher has a white spot on his chest and has ruffled feathers and why the gulls are Noble Scratchers. Stories of Manabozo (also Manabozho) or Nanabush (also Manabush) are widespread among many Amerindian peoples.

The ancient belief is that a manitou or god visited earth and fell in love with a maiden. He made her his wife, and their first son was Manabozo.

The Algonquian, Chippewa, and Menomini call the great hare Manabozo or Manabush, and the Menomini say Manabozo was born a little white rabbit.

In modern times, the god has become a trickster hero. Manabozo arranged the hunting relationship between men and animals so people would have enough to eat. His grandmother brought death into the world so the earth wouldn't become overcrowded. When she did this, Hare took his blanket and covered himself with it. He then lay down in a corner and wept for human beings who must die. It was then he thought of creating the medicine rite.

The Chippewa say the medicine rite was given to Manabozo by the spirits to console him for the loss of Wolf. The medicine rite is concerned with death and reincarnation. In one sense, Manabozo, swallowed by the fish, symbolically dies and is reborn again when the gulls set him free.

Ajidaumo is a complimentary name given to the squirrel because the squirrel is said to be an animal that respects anything dead and will not feed upon it. Note that Ajidaumo does not eat any of the dead fish, as the gulls do.

The Horned Women

The woman of the house sat up all alone, as the rest of her family slept. It was long into the night, and she was deep in her work of combing and preparing wool for spinning.

All at once, there was a hard, fast tapping at her door. "You must open. Open!" said a voice.

"Who calls? Who is there?" the house woman asked.

"I am the witch of one horn," came the reply.

Well, the woman wasn't sure what she had heard. And thinking it might be her neighbor wanting help, she opened the door. At once, an old woman came in. And in her hand she held two wool carders, not unlike the one the woman of the house had been using to card and comb her wool fibers. The stranger who entered had a horn growing right in the middle of her forehead.

Silently, the horned woman sat down before the fire. She started carding the wool in a great rush.

"Where are the other women?" she asked the house woman. "They are taking too much time."

There was another knock now at the door. A voice called again, "You must open. Open!"

The house woman opened the door. A second witch was standing there. She had two horns in the middle of her forehead, and she carried a wheel for spinning wool.

Entering, she said, "Make room. I am the witch of the two horns." At once, she began spinning.

All night, the knocks at the door came. The call was made, the witches all came in.

There were twelve of them at last, all sitting around the fire. There was the first one who had one horn. And counting to the last, there was one who had twelve horns.

They carded the wool fiber, they spun the wool on their spinning wheels, and they sang a very old rhyme all the while. Not once did they give a nod or speak again to the woman of the house.

The women were ugly and strange, what with their horns and spinning wheels. The woman of the house was frightened out of her wits. She couldn't move nor cry out, for the witches had placed their spell on her.

Toward dawn, one witch said to her, "Get up, woman, and make us a cake."

The woman moved to get a bowl to fetch some well water so she could mix the meal and make a cake; but she dropped three bowls, she was so full of terror.

"Take a sieve, then," the witches said. "Fetch water in a sieve."

The house woman took a sieve made of tiny mesh openings and went to the well. But water fell through the mesh; she couldn't keep it for the cake. And she cried then, kneeling there by the well.

There was a voice next to her suddenly. "Take clay and moss," it said. It was no other than the Spirit of the Well. "Plaster them over the sieve, and it will hold water."

The house woman did this, and the sieve held water for the cake.

"Go home now," the Spirit spoke again.

So the house woman went back to her home with the water. She gave it to the witches who mixed it with meal and a bit of blood they'd taken from each member of her sleeping family.

While they were so awfully busy, the house woman heard the Spirit of the Well call to her. "Go to the north corner of your house," it said. "Cry out three times: 'The mountain of the horned women and the sky above it are on fire!'"

Well, the house woman did this. When the witches heard her call, they screamed and rushed all around. They wailed and moaned loudly. And then they left as mysteriously as they had come.

The Spirit of the Well spoke once more to the house woman. It told her how to fix her house against witchery, for the Spirit knew the horned witches would return again.

The house woman sprinkled her child's feet water outside the door. Yes, it was the very same water she had used for bathing her child's feet.

She found the cake the witches had made of meal and water mixed with the bit of blood taken from her sleeping family. She broke the cake in little pieces and placed a piece in each sleeper's mouth. They had been under the witches' spells.

The house woman took the cloth the witches had woven and put it in a chest and locked it. Finally, she closed the door with a huge log, forcing it in the doorjambs. The witches could never enter through it.

Then the house woman waited.

Soon the witches came back. They were in a rage, and they threw curses all around.

"Open, you!" they screeched. "Feet water, let us pass!"

"Oh, no, indeed," said the child's feet water. "I am all on the ground. I am seeping down on my way to the sea."

"Open you, door log!" the witches cried to the door.

"No, indeed," said the door. "The log is there in the jambs, and I will stay tight shut."

"Let us in, the cake we made," said the witches.

"No, I won't," said the cake. "I've been broken in pieces, and my blood kissed the lips of those who slept. Now the spell on them is broken in pieces, too."

The witches rushed away to where witches all go. And they cursed the Spirit of the Well who caused their ruin. The house woman was left alone with her good family at last.

One of the wild witches had dropped her cloak in her hurry to be gone. For years and years the family kept this dark cloak hanging on the wall. It hung for generations, so it is told. And for five hundred years more, in shreds and strings, as fair warning to all horned witches.

COMMENT

This is an ancient Irish legend, parts of which can be found in many other stories. In another tale, "The Well at the World's End," a girl attempts to fill a sieve with water only to have the water leak out again. A frog tells the girl to daub the sieve with clay; she does, and the water stays in the sieve. This "sieve bucket task" is spread worldwide from the Greeks to one of the Bruh Rabbit stories recorded by Joel Chandler Harris in the American South — "Fill it [the sieve] wid moss en dob it wid clay."[1]

In an earlier version, the witches in the above story were called Fenian Women. In Irish legend these were the women of Fenians, the group of warriors under the leadership of Finn McCaul (sometimes written Fionn MacCumal), who were always ready to defend Ireland.

[1]From *Uncle Remus: His Songs and His Sayings* by Joel Chandler Harris

The Flying Dutchman

Long ago there lived a Dutch sea captain called Van-der-decken. His ship was named the *Flying Dutchman*. One time, during a heavy storm, Captain Vanderdecken was trying to take his ship around the Cape of Good Hope at the tip of Africa. But the weather was black and thick with fog. The *Flying Dutchman* made no progress at all.

"I swear to God," the captain cried, "I shall double round the Cape no matter what length of time it takes. I'll be damned if I don't!"

Well, God himself had been listening. At once, he appeared before Captain Vanderdecken.

"Stop what you are doing!" God said. His holy voice spread over the waters. "You have used my name as a curse, you have sworn it."

But the captain was stubborn; he wouldn't stop. He refused to heed God, and he drew his pistol. He shot at God! Yet the bullet went wide.

Captain Vanderdecken was so angry God had interfered that he tried to hit him with his fist. Foolish man! His arm fell without strength.

God cursed the captain in words of wisdom and eternity.

"From this day onward," spoke God to Vanderdecken, "you shall wander the sea and every ocean. You shall never reach any port.

"You will have foul weather forever," said God. "You will have chill winds and gales to stay with you. You will drink bitterness; you will never sleep.

"Man of the sea," God swore, "your body shall grow deformed. You will become hated as the Devil of the oceans. Whenever you are seen by a passing ship, a disaster will strike those who see you."

So it was that God took all hope away from sailors, he did. And then, at last, he returned to his heaven.

"I dare you!" the captain shouted after God. "I dare you!" he cried, shaking his fists. "I challenge you. I resist you!"

Poor fool, that Captain Vanderdecken. Not only did his wandering ship, the *Flying Dutchman,* bring storms, but some say to this very day the ship brings the plague and madness, too. No one can board it. It glows like a ghostly specter of its former self. It has no sails now and no sides or deck. Just ribs, like a skeleton. It has no live crew. Its figurehead is a skeleton, and skeleton men swarm over it. It sails through the air and backwards, too.

For all time, the spirit of the foolish captain warns sailors of what is to come. Just before a violent storm or when fog or snow or sleet falls heavily on the sea like a shroud, a passing ship crosses the *Flying Dutchman*'s course. The crew sees *Dutchman* and a ghostly captain; but

then it is too late. The passing ship has caught the *Dutchman*'s curse; it loses its mainmast in high seas. It hits something unseen and sinks with all its crew, without a trace.

So then, heed this heartfelt song of sailors:

"But Heaven help the ship near which the demon sailor steers, —
The doom of those is sealed, to whom that Phantom Ship
appears:
They'll never reach their destined port, —
they'll see their homes no more, —
They who see the Flying Dutchman — never, never reach the
shore!"[1]

The drowned of the passing ship join the crew of *Dutchman,* don't you know. They wander to the end of time, collecting other drowned of the oceans. They cannot die as we do. They cannot go ashore but must toil on and on forever.

Sailors who have heard this tale told time and time again know the truth of it. For they sail no more; they stay at home. And sleep at night!

COMMENT

"The Flying Dutchman" is the most famous of the popular legends about phantom ships and is of both Dutch and German origin. The ship is said to haunt the waters around the Cape of Good Hope, and the sighting of it means quick disaster. The common version of the legend above is the basis for the opera *Der Fliegende Holländer* by the German composer Richard Wagner, which premiered in Dresden in 1843.

In a similar legend, a Reginald Falkenberg sails forever through the North Sea playing dice with the Devil, who wants his soul.

The wandering motif is found worldwide in stories about a legendary character who must roam without rest because of curses or actions against divine beings.

[1]From "The Flying Dutchman" by John Boyle O'Reilly

Medusa

She was a lovely young woman, was Me-du-sa. She liked herself better than she cared for anyone else. She thought highly of her own good looks, particularly her profile and her long golden hair rippling in waves to her waist.

"There is no goddess on high as beautiful as I am," bragged Medusa.

Just then, Athena, the Goddess of Wisdom, happened by and heard Medusa's boast.

"Medusa, I don't like the sound of that," she said. "From now on, no man shall look at you and think you are beautiful."

At once, the goddess changed Medusa into a monstrous Gorgon. Medusa's golden hair became a tangle of hideous, hissing snakes. Then and forever, whoever looked at Medusa was turned to stone.

Indeed, because of Athena's curse, the whole countryside in which Medusa dwelled was nearly laid waste. Statues, former humans, littered the landscape. For anyone looking upon the horrid head of Medusa was turned into cold stone.

At this time there lived one Per-se-us, the sun prince. He had been adopted by Poly-dec-tes, who was the king. Polydectes hoped to win Perseus's mother, Danae, as his wife. The king could be kind or cruel, depending on the mood he was in. He was jealous of Perseus's good looks and Danae's affection for him. Polydectes hoped to find a way to get rid of him.

Perseus grew up, wishing to show the king how grateful he was to him. "Whatever you wish, I will get for you," he told the king. "Name what you will, and it is yours."

Polydectes had an inspiration. "Bring me the head of Medusa," said the king, "for she destroys my kingdom."

Perseus was shocked. Everyone knew about Medusa, and no man dared look at her or take a weapon to her head.

Perseus felt very alone. Not knowing what else to do, he went down to the sea to think. He sat with his head in his hands. A fisherman nearby asked him what was the matter.

"The king wants me to bring him the head of Medusa," said Perseus.

"Almost an impossible task," the fisherman said. "But I have something that might help you." He reached out; as if by magic, he took a pouch from the air. Suddenly the fisherman's clothing vanished, and he wore a silver breastplate. The cap he wore changed into a golden helmet. A light glowed all around the man.

"I . . . I recognize you! You are no fisherman," stammered Perseus. "You are the god Hermes."

"I am," said Hermes. "All know me as the son and messenger of the gods. We are both the sons of the god Zeus. Zeus has watched you grow and become a strong young man. He won't let harm come to you."

"But what am I to do?" asked Perseus. "How can I behead Medusa without turning to stone myself?"

"You can do it," said the god, "but you will need three things: a brass shield as bright as a mirror, a pair of sandals that will let you fly, and a sword so sharp it will cut through anything in a single stroke."

"Where will I find these things?" asked Perseus.

"Go to the rim of the world," said Hermes. "There you will find three women born gray and wrinkled. They are called the Graeae, and they have one eye and one tooth among them. The Graeae know where the things you need are hidden.

"They won't tell you unless you can persuade them to, or make them do it somehow," said Hermes. "Perseus, you must not hurt them. But be clever. Now go and see what happens."

A long time passed before Perseus came to the rim of the world. And in that twilight land he found the Graeae.

"I sense a man coming near," said the first gray woman.

"I hear him walking," said the second gray woman.

"Now we will look at him," said the last gray woman.

"Pass us the eye so we may see," said the first two. When the last gray woman handed them the eye, Perseus snatched it away.

"Oh, our eye is stolen! We cannot see. Oh, give it back!" cried the Graeae.

"I will give it back if you help me," said Perseus. "I must find a brass shield as bright as a mirror, a pair of sandals that will let me fly, and a sword so sharp it will cut through anything."

"We swore to keep what you desire a secret," said the first gray woman.

"But now we cannot see and are helpless," cried the second.

"So we will tell you. Listen!" said the third.

Perseus listened as the hags told all: "Travel to the south till you come to an island with a black peak high above the water. You will find a cave at the foot of the peak. In the cave, under a stone slab, are the objects you wish."

Perseus hurried away. Days later he found the cave and the objects where the gray women said he would. He took the sword and shield in one hand and put the sandals on with the other. Then he flew away on the air.

Perseus saw Medusa seated at the very summit of the black peak. All around were fallen birds and animals, and dead men who had been turned to stone. He dared not look at Medusa but watched her image reflected on his shield. Flying swiftly near, he cut through Medusa's head of snakes with one blow. Perseus put her head in the pouch Hermes had given him. Then he flew home.

"So," said the king on his return, "you've come back with something for me?"

"I have what you asked for in this pouch," Perseus answered.

"Show me!" commanded the king.

Perseus opened the pouch and held up the awful head of Medusa. Her lifeless eyes were wide open in a deadly stare. The king was so shocked he could not turn away. Slowly he stiffened in agony. With a look of horror, Polydectes turned to stone. And there the hard king sits, a statue still.

COMMENT

In some versions of this story, King Polydectes is cruelhearted, and he persecutes Perseus's mother, Danae, who refuses to marry him. His hatefulness to Danae may be the reason Perseus shows him the Medusa head.

Medusa is said to be one of three Gorgons — the winged monsters who were covered in golden scales and had snakes for hair. They were related to the Graeae. Medusa was the only Gorgon born a mortal, and, therefore, she could be killed.

Early Romans received their science and religion from the ancient Greeks. Although the beliefs of both are extinct, their mythology lives through the stories of the gods.

Thus, the Roman god Mercury is akin to the Greek god Hermes and was the messenger of the gods. His father, Jupiter, is also similar to the Greek supreme god, Zeus. Athena is the Greek version of Minerva. After Perseus slew Medusa, her head was mounted on the aegis, or "shield," of Zeus.

The Wicked Stepmother

A blowing wind knows when to stop. But a wicked woman never quits her evil. So the story is told, and here it begins.

Long ago in Russia, a woman lived with her old husband and with a stepdaughter and one daughter of her own. The mother always praised her own daughter, who was ugly and as mean as her mother. She never praised her stepdaughter, although the maiden was so good and sweet.

One day the stepmother told her husband, "Take your daughter out of my sight. Don't take her to your relatives and a warm hut; take her into the fields — to the frost that cracks from cold."

The old father hung his head with sadness. "I cannot do such a thing!" he cried.

"Do it," demanded his wife, "or your child will be sorry!"

The husband nearly wept. But he did as he was told. He put his lovely daughter in his sleigh. He did not even dare to cover her with a quilt, for the stepmother watched from the window. The father took the young girl into the snowfields and left her there all alone. He hurried away in the sleigh. He could not bear to watch his daughter freeze out in the cold.

His daughter was brokenhearted and afraid. And she spoke every prayer she knew.

All at once, a great being appeared out of the cold and ice. He was tall and thin. He wore fine furs from head to foot. His beard was long and white. His jeweled crown sparkled on his white head. Indeed, he was the sovereign king of the snowfields. He was Father Frost.

Father Frost stared down at the beautiful, shivering girl and asked, "Do you know who I am? Do you know this mighty Frost of the red, red nose and icy brows?"

"Oh, yes, sire," spoke the stepdaughter. "Father Frost, be welcome here while I wait to die."

"I hope you are comfortable, sweet girl," said Father Frost.

"Oh, yes, I am," she said, breathlessly, for the cold caught in her throat and slowly froze her inside.

Frost, who was so bright all around, noted how well she spoke and how sweet she was. He shone in the branches until they cracked. He filled the air until it floated with glistening ice.

The stepdaughter said again and again, "I am comfortable, Father Frost, I am well."

Father Frost was charmed by the stepdaughter. "She is different," he thought. And he gave her a trunk full of beautiful gowns. He presented her with a cloak lined with fur. He gave her silken quilts that were warm but light in weight. He gave her a blue sarafan, the national

costume, with silver and pearl ornaments. The girl was now rich and looked like a queen dressed in the fine clothing.

Back home, the stepmother was busy making pancakes to be eaten following the prayer service for the dead stepdaughter.

"Go down to the fields and bring back your dead daughter so we can bury her," the stepmother told her husband.

He went off then with his head bowed low. The woman's little dog sat there in the kitchen and watched him go. The dog started wagging his tail and barked: "Bowwow! Ruff-ruff! The poor father's daughter is coming home. She's as happy as she's never been. But the stepmother's daughter is as wicked as she's *ever* been."

The woman was angry, and she whipped the dog, but that didn't stop his tail wagging and tale telling. So she gave him some pancakes; and they never stopped him either.

The gate opened. The stepmother heard voices laughing and talking there. She saw her stepdaughter who had come home looking like a princess. The young woman wore fine clothes, and her father could hardly drag the heavy trunk, spilling its treasure everywhere.

"Old man," said the stepmother, calling out the door. "Hitch the horses to the sleigh. Drive *my* wonderful daughter to the same place in the snowfields." So the poor man did as he was told and took the woman's daughter to the place he'd left his own daughter. And then he went back home as fast as he could go.

Father Frost came there. He saw the young woman. "And are you comfortable, sweet maiden?" asked Frost.

"Oh, you leave me alone!" said the girl, as meanly as she could. "Don't you see how cold and stiff my feet have become from the cold?"

Frost kept on questioning and crackling all around. And never did the girl give him a kind word or a smile. So Father Frost froze the girl to her death.

Back home, the stepmother was shouting to her husband, as usual. "You! Go find my daughter and bring her back. And watch out, don't overturn the sleigh and lose the trunk."

So the poor man set out again. The little dog wagged his tail and barked: "Bowwow, ruff-ruff! The poor man's daughter will soon be married. The old woman's daughter will soon be buried."

"Hush, don't say such things!" said the woman. "Eat this cake and tell me, 'the woman's daughter is dressed in royal clothes fit for a wedding.'" But the dog would never bark those words.

Then the gate creaked. The stepmother ran outside. She saw that her daughter was cold and dead. "Oh! Oh!" she cried. She kissed her daughter's ice-cold lips. She moaned and sobbed. But there was no help for her daughter whose face was frozen in a frown.

So the story is told, and here it ends.

COMMENT

This is a cautionary story from old Russia, in which the wicked stepmother learns something of value the hard way. It is the Jack Frost form of tale; the motif is one of reward and punishment, kindness and churlishness, in which a mean person does not listen to an animal's warnings. The person is punished for not heeding the truth told by the animal—in this instance, a dog. The good person, the stepdaughter, is kind. Father Frost rewards her. The daughter of the cruel stepmother is punished by Frost when she is harsh and impolite. In some versions of the tale, the dog's barking announces that the good stepdaughter will wed the king.

The Tiny Thing

Some tell of a man all alone, and his name was A-ni-shin-aba. He had nothing better to do than go here, go there. He searched for a friend until he was too tired to go on. Anishinaba stretched out on the ground and was soon asleep.

At dawn, he heard a voice in his dreams calling: "My grandchild! My grandchild!"

Anishinaba woke up with a start. "Who is calling me?" he thought. He looked all around.

Finally, he saw a tiny thing, hardly big enough to see. It was an animal of some sort, and it cried out again. "I am Bosh-kwa-dosh. Do you hear me, my grandson? Why are you so all alone? If you listen well, you will be happy. Tie me to you and never put me down. Then, for all of your life there will be goodness with you."

Well, the man thought all this sounded fine. He took up the tiny animal. The only hair on the creature was at the very tip of its tail. Otherwise, it was bald as it could be and the size of a newborn mouse.

Anishinaba put Boshkwadosh in a little sack as carefully as he could. He put the sack on a sash and bound it around his waist. And then he set out, looking for someone. He walked a long way; he saw neither man nor beast. But just beyond the hill he climbed, there was a town and a single road through it. The lodges on one side of the road seemed empty, while on the other side, people were living in the lodges there.

Anishinaba went into the town; the people came out. Then the chief's son appeared. He greeted Anishinaba kindly. He took Anishinaba to his father's lodge, and the chief brought out his beautiful daughter to meet Anishinaba.

Anishinaba married the daughter. He rested there among the people and later joined in their games and trials. They asked him to make the trial of the frost, and they told him how to do it.

Out from the village was a frozen lake. Anishinaba, with two companions, went there and lay down, without any clothes, on the ice. But Anishinaba did not take off his sash. He and the two companions lay with their faces upon the ice. They would find out who could brave the ice the longest.

There was much laughing and calling to Anishinaba from the other two. But he never answered them. There was a warmth that came from his sash where tiny Boshkwadosh was hidden, and Anishinaba knew he would be all right.

Much later in the night, he spoke to the two friends. They had been silent for a long time. "And are you so numb you cannot talk?" he asked. "I, Anishinaba, only now feel the cold."

There was no answer. Anishinaba waited until daybreak; then he went over to his companions. They were quite cold and dead. He was amazed to find they had been changed into buffalo. Quickly, he tied them together and carried them back to the village.

The chief was pleased with his success. The people were not; their loved ones had died in the cold and were placed in the silent lodges on the side of the road where nobody lived. The death lodges.

Anishinaba was given another trial. This one was of speed, and he did well. He ran faster than everyone — as though he had the wings of the sparrow hawk.

The villagers asked him to repeat the trial of frost. Always obliging, Anishinaba agreed. First, he lay down to rest. He untied his sash and placed it beneath his head. He slept for a long time; when he awoke, he got up in too much of a hurry. You see, he was feeling strong. He ran to the ice and did not remember he had taken off the sash with tiny Boshkwadosh inside the little sack.

Anishinaba lay down on the ice. But now there was nothing to keep the cold away. By the dawn, he was frozen, stiff and dead.

The chief was greatly saddened. His daughter, Anishinaba's wife, couldn't stop crying. Lying sobbing in her lodge, she heard groans and sighs from somewhere. They went on all night. The next day, she searched for what might have made the sorrowful sounds and found Anishinaba's sash.

"You! Untie me!" cried something inside the sack there on the sash. The wife opened the sack and found the little animal. The tiny thing

was very weak. It would crawl and rest, crawl and rest. Each time it rested, it would shake itself. And each time it shook, it grew!

Soon, Boshkwadosh was a large dog. He ran to gather Anishinaba's bones. These had been scattered in the silent lodges. Boshkwadosh put them in order, making a skeleton out of them. He stood over them and howled in a low, long sound. The bones seemed to pull together. Boshkwadosh howled a second time, louder, and the bones held tightly to each other. He howled again, and tendons and muscles wrapped around the bones. He howled softly, and then flesh came and covered the bones.

Boshkwadosh lifted his face to the above. The howl he gave up made the earth shake. It made the people so afraid they trembled.

Anishinaba breathed; he came to life. "I must have overslept," he said. "I'm going to be late for my trial."

"Oh, say!" said Boshkwadosh. "You forgot me and left me behind, so you were beaten at the game. You froze to death. Yet with my power, I brought you back to life. And I shall now show you who I am."

So it was that this mystery in the shape of a dog began to shake itself again and again. It grew large. *Shake! Shake!* It grew into a giant and seemed to touch the sky.

"If I showed my greatest power," said Boshkwadosh, "I would fill the world, and everything on earth could not feed my hunger. So I shall not show all of my strength; I will give some of it to you.

"Anishinaba," spoke the great giant, "animals belong to me, and I say that from now on, animals belong to you. They shall be your food."

Then the mysterious being, Boshkwadosh, disappeared forever.

COMMENT

This is an inspired legend of the plains Amerindians, one of many showing that the seeds of life were thought to be contained in human and animal bones. We are introduced to the mythic personage, Boshkwadosh, and the ritual of trials. Death and rebirth here are symbolic rites of passage — the initiation into adulthood. Community rites are mingled with Anishinaba's, who is himself in search of a guardian spirit.

The little sack worn on Anishinaba's sash represents the magic medicine sack. Members of the tribe wore medicine sack amulets holding animal bones, and sometimes feathers and other objects thought to have power. This magic of the bones allowed their keeper to pass through all things — even a tree or a rock.

The Pretender

He was honored. He came as the pretender, so they say. He was the likeness and spirit of Tez-cat-li-poca, Smoking Mirror, the creator and destroyer god. He was chosen to stand for the god because he was handsome and quick. He was clean and fair, long, lean, and well built.

The pretender had no flaw. The emperor Montezuma adorned him in golden clothing. The pretender's face was blackened. Soft, white eagle feathers were put on his head. He had a crown of flowers and a mantle of flowers, as well. Carved gold and shell pendants hung from his ears. Into his ears went turquoise plugs. He wore a shell necklace and a white seashell breast ornament.

Golden bracelets fitted on his upper arms, and carved ones of precious stones circled his wrists. A cape of fishnet was put over him. His loincloth reached from his waist to his calves. Golden bells were placed on his feet. When he ran, he went ringing and jingling all the way. His sandals were fashioned from ocelot ear skin.

He was taught the flute, to play it well. He held bunches of flowers and carried a spear. He blew and sucked on his smoking tube, and he smelled the flowers. That was the way the pretender went walking, dressed in finery, with his flute, flowers, smoking tube, and spear.

He lived in the house with his guardian. Before the people saw him he was taught how to speak with grace, how to greet them nicely if he happened to come upon them as he walked.

The pretender lived this way for one year. He walked, playing his flute. Night and day he did as he pleased. He had eight young men following him and four warriors. They taught him the art of war.

The pretender was the lord god; all treated him as a lord is treated — begging favors. The common people bowed in praise, kissing the ground. He led the way, he cast the spear. For one year he gave commands, for he had been chosen by the temple guardians to do this, to be the lord god. He was the one-and-only out of all they had taught and cared for.

And for twelve months, the pretender lived as high as a god; he was a god. He played his flute, smoked his smoking tube, and he did whatever he wished.

Twenty days before the feast of Smoking Mirror was held, the pretender was married to four girls who were dressed as goddesses. He took off all of his ornaments. He fasted and was painted black. His hair was cut. He had a tuft of hair tied on his forehead. He had a forked heron-feather ornament with single quetzal (ket-zel) feathers attached to his hair.

Five days before the feast, in the month of Toxcatl (Tox-ca-tl), the pretender's guard brought food for the people. Everyone sang and danced for four days. Afterwards, on the last day, the pretender went in a canoe with his wives. They kept him in good spirits with their laughter until the canoe arrived at the shore.

Next, the pretender went on alone, with only his guards to accompany him. When he arrived at a small temple, he went up the steps by himself. It was his free will, you see, that made him go. He climbed the first step, passed it, and shattered his flute and broke his spear also.

And when the pretender reached the top, the priests were waiting. They grabbed him, they threw him on his back upon the stone of sacrifice. One priest cut open his chest. *Ahhhhhg!* Swiftly, the priest seized the pretender's beating heart and raised it high to the sun. The great sun would surely die unless it was fed with human heart blood.

Four men carried the pretender's body down. His head was cut off his body. It was strung there on a skull rack. And so he ended his royal reign, this brave pretender. He was dead in honor and glory. He who had been low, who became a god for one year, died a great death.

COMMENT

In Mexican mythology this legend is a dramatization of an annual ritual of the Aztecs, when in ancient times, a warrior prisoner became the pretender, or symbol of the god, and was sacrificed to the god Tezcatlipoca. The cult of Tezcatlipoca and human sacrifice was brought to central Mexico by the Toltecs, the Nahuatl-speaking warriors from the north, at the end of the tenth century A.D. The twenty days before the sacrifice symbolized the winter solstice. It was thought that the sun, in its subterranean world, feared for its freedom for its light had been imprisoned by the darkness of

winter. The pretender's death represented the liberation of the sun. The symbolic spirit of Tezcatlipoca was then reborn at once into the body of another youth who would be the pretender until he, too, was put to death at the feast the next year.

Myths tell how the god expelled the priest-king and later, Quetzalcóatl, the Green-Feathered Serpent, the god of wind and master of life, from his center at Tula. Tezcatlipoca's nagual, or animal disguise, was the jaguar, the spotted skin of which was compared to the stars in the sky and the constellations.

A quetzal is a brilliantly colored bird, one species of which is the national emblem of Guatamala.

Childe Rowland and Burd Ellen

This tale comes from long, long ago. There were fairies then — some ugly, some lovely, some good, and some awful. There were elves, much like fairies, and dwarfs and pixies, all living in the land of Fairy, which some call Elfland, too.

Childe Rowland was a noble boy and part of a human family. His mother was the queen. One day, he and his two older brothers and his sister, Burd Ellen, were out kicking a ball about. Rowland kicked it so high it sailed over the church. Burd Ellen went chasing after it on the church's other side. She never came back.

The brothers searched everywhere for Burd Ellen, but she had vanished. Finally, the oldest of the brothers went to the cave where the enchanter, Merlin, lived. Merlin said Burd Ellen must have been carried off by fairies.

"She had to have gone round the church widdershins," said Merlin. "And that means 'going the opposite way than the sun moves.' It surely is the cause of this fairy mischief."

"But can we get my sister back?" asked the brother.

"Oh, it's possible," great Merlin said, "but you must be taught how."

"Then teach me, oh, please!" begged the eldest brother. "I'll do it or die trying."

So it was that Merlin taught him what to do. And the eldest brother set out for the land of fairies.

The family waited long, long times, but the eldest brother never returned.

The second-oldest brother went to Merlin, asking to be taught. When he had learned all that the eldest brother had, he set out to find Burd Ellen and his brother.

The family waited long, long times. But this brother, also, never returned.

Childe Rowland, the youngest, wished to go in search of Burd Ellen and her brothers. He went to his mother, the queen, to ask permission.

"Oh, but you are dear to me!" she told him. "I fear you will be lost!"

Childe Rowland begged and begged. At last, the queen gave in. "I give you your father's sword," she said. "It never failed him."

Childe Rowland put it through his belt. The queen said a spell over it to bring him triumph.

"Farewell, Mother!" said Childe Rowland. He went to Merlin's cave. "How may I rescue my sister and my brothers?" Rowland asked.

"There are two things—one to do, and one not to do," Merlin told him.

"And they are?" asked Rowland.

"The thing to do is this," said Merlin. "When you enter the Fairy-Elf land, cut off anyone's head who speaks to you before you meet Burd Ellen."

"And the thing not to do?" asked Childe Rowland.

Said Merlin, "No matter how thirsty or hungry you become, take no drink of anything, nor eat anything while in Fairy-Elf land, or you will never see home again."

Childe Rowland learned the two things by heart, one to do, and one not to do. After thanking Merlin, he went on his way until he came upon the horsekeeper for the elf king of Fairy.

"Ah, at last I am among them!" thought Childe Rowland. And he said to the keeper, "Where is the Dark Tower of the king?"

"I do not know," said the keeper. "Go farther and find the cowherd. He may know."

Childe Rowland said no more. He drew the sword that had never failed his father, and he chopped off the horsekeeper's head.

Childe Rowland went farther on. Soon he met the herder of cows and asked him the question.

"I don't know about the Dark Tower nor its king," said the cowherd. "Go farther until you meet an old woman in a gray shawl. She is the henkeeper. Surely she will know."

Childe Rowland pulled out his father's sword that had never failed him and toppled the cowherd's head.

He went on farther until he saw the old woman wearing a gray shawl.

"Do you know where to find the Dark Tower of the king of Fairy?" he asked.

"Go farther," said the henkeeper. "You will come to a green hill stepped with terraces up and down. Go round the hill three times, widdershins. Each time you must say this: 'Door! Door! Open, open! Let me come in.' The third time, the door will open, and you can go in."

Childe Rowland took out his sword that never failed his father, and off went the henkeeper's old gray head. Then he went on until he came to the terraced hill. He went round it three times, widdershins.

And he said: "Door! Door! Open, open! Let me come in."

The third time, the door opened. Childe Rowland went in, he did. The door closed behind him, and he was in the dark.

The dark was like evening, like dusk or twilight. The air was warm, as it always is in the land of Fairy. He walked in shadows, seeing a great hall before him.

He passed through folding doors and found himself in a place of diamonds and emeralds. Five pillars of silver and gold were entwined with clusters of flowers made of rubies and pearls. The furnishings were magical and grand.

On a huge couch of velvet and silk sat Burd Ellen. She was combing her yellow hair with a silver comb.

When she saw her brother, Burd Ellen cried out, "Oh, woe! Oh, sadness, you cannot save me, Childe Rowland; you cannot save anyone. Be sorry you were ever born. The king of Fairy will surely catch you and eat you!"

They sat down together, and Childe Rowland told Burd Ellen all that had happened and what he had done. She told him that their brothers came to the Dark Tower and were captured by the king. Now they lay as though dead.

Childe Rowland said he was hungry and asked for food. He forgot all about Merlin's warning. Burd Ellen was under a spell and could not tell her brother not to eat. She brought him bread and milk.

Just as he was about to drink the milk, she managed to shake her head. Childe Rowland saw and suddenly remembered what he must not do.

Not to eat, he recalled, *not one bite, until Burd Ellen is free at last!*

All at once, a booming voice broke through the quiet of the enormous room:

> "Fee, fi, fo, fum —
>   I smell the blood of a nobleman.
>   Be he dead, be he living,
>   With my sword in hand,
>   I will slice his brains
>   From his brain pan."

The folding doors burst open. There stood a dreadful creature, so huge and green, with pointy ears and mighty hands and feet. Oh, it was the giant of the Dark Tower, himself. It was the elf king of Fairy.

Childe Rowland pulled out the sword that had never failed his father, nor him. The giant and the brave boy slashed at one another. Their swords clanged, and they fought all day. At last Childe Rowland beat the elf king to his knees.

"I'll spare you if you break my sister's spell and bring my brothers to life again," he said.

"So be it," said the giant elf king. He rubbed red ointment on the eyes and lips and fingertips of the two brothers. They came to life at once. The king murmured something to Burd Ellen. She shuddered and then smiled, wide awake.

With Childe Rowland, his sister and his brothers fled the Dark Tower, never to return.

When they at last reached home, the queen was waiting. She embraced them, her brave children. They all laughed and cried from happiness.

Sweet Burd Ellen had learned her lesson. Never again did she go around the church, widdershins.

COMMENT

This is a common story of the English Middle Ages. Its sources are Scandinavian, Scottish, Celtic, and English.

Childe (Rowland) means "youth of noble birth." Burd (Ellen) is "a female, a wellborn lady." Widdershins was a term used in the sixteenth century. It is a corruption of withershins, a Scottish word meaning "to go in the opposite direction from the natural one." To go counterclockwise, especially contrary to the course of the sun, to go widdershins, was considered very unlucky, the cause of certain disaster.

The term Elfland came into use in the fifteenth century. Fairy Land or the land of Fairy (or Faerie) was used more than a century later. In versions of the above story, the terms are interchangeable.

Everlasting Life

There is a maiden who holds a magic lotus blossom in her hand. She plays upon the reed organ, making a sweet and delicate sound. The maiden's name is Ho Hsien ku, and she is the daughter of a shopkeeper in Hunan.

When she was born, she had only six hairs growing from her head. Never did she have any more, so they say. She lived atop a mountain where there are stones called Yun-mu shih — mother-of-pearl.

Ho Hsien ku dreamed about a spirit. The spirit told her to eat one of the Yun-mu shih stones. If she did, she would have grace and everlasting life.

The maiden ate the stone. Slowly, very slowly, she then lost the desire to eat. She lost weight and felt herself lifting on the air. Soon she spent each day floating from one mountain peak to the next. At night she

would bring her dear mother all of the fruits and herbs she had picked as she floated about.

After a time, Ho Hsien ku found she didn't need to eat to stay alive. She was immortal, and she did not need food. She would exist forever.

Ho Hsien ku's fame spread. The Empress Wu Hou[1] heard about her and invited the maiden to her castle. While making the journey to the royal court, Ho Hsien ku vanished from the sight of human beings. But they say she was seen again fifty years later. Someone saw her floating on a cloud full of rainbows. It was at the temple of the famous woman magician, Ma Ku, that this took place.

Years later, Ho Hsien ku was seen floating again in the city of Canton. And to this day, she is thought of as a most high Immortal.

One time, she and the other seven Immortals declared war on and defeated the evil Dragon-king of the Eastern Sea over the theft of one of their musical instruments. The Immortals are known to have many pleasant adventures. Indeed they are called Pa-Hsien, which has come to mean "happiness." Their number, eight, is always lucky.

COMMENT

In Chinese mythology Ho Hsien ku is one of the Eight Immortals of the Taoist religion and the only female. As a girl she dreamed that mother-of-pearl brought immortality. She ate some and became lighter than air. Artists depict her as a beautiful woman holding a lotus flower.

[1] Seventh century A.D.

Tanuki Magic Teakettle

It is told, there was a holy man living at the temple. He found pleasure in the ancient tea ceremony. One day, he uncovered a rusty old kettle in a musty shop at the edge of his village.

"It is not so worn-out that it can't be made better," he said, holding the dented iron pot to the light. "I will have this, if you please," he told the shopkeeper.

The holy man bought the kettle and took it home. He sat himself comfortably and hammered out the dents. Then he polished the old kettle until it was shining like new.

"Look what I have here," he said to his pupils who came to have tea with him.

"What a fine-looking new kettle," one of them said.

The holy man smiled at that. Only he knew how very old and rusted had been the shiny teakettle. He put the kettle on the charcoal hibachi stove. He and his pupils sat waiting as the kettle grew hot. "Rrrrrm. RrrRRM," went the kettle, as it heated. "RRRRRMM!"

Suddenly, there was a shout: "Ouch! Ouch!"

The holy man jumped from his seat. "What was that?" he asked.

Before any of his pupils could answer, the new old teakettle began spinning around. "Oh, it's hot! Help! Get me out!" cried the teakettle.

The holy man and his pupils scrambled away. All at once, the teakettle sprouted a head with a narrow face. It grew a long bushy tail. It had the perfect little feet of a small, furry animal, a tanuki (tah-noo-kee).

"Fire! Fire!" yelped the tanuki. "My insides are burning!"

The tanuki teakettle jumped straight up from the charcoal blaze and began racing around the room. "Help! Oh, help!" it moaned.

Well, the holy man and his pupils tried to catch it, but the teakettle was too swift for them. The tanuki kettle leaped here and there, knocking over boxes and screens as it scurried every which way.

At last, a pupil caught it and flung it inside a box. Just then, the tanuki teakettle's bushy tail, its head, and four tiny feet vanished. The jumping, yelling thing — part iron pot, part animal — became a common teakettle again.

"I think the teakettle is bewitched," said the holy man in a hushed voice. "And I do not believe such magic should stay with us in this temple."

It happened that a tinker passed the temple every other day. The next time he passed, the holy man had the teakettle ready. "You may have this teakettle," he said to the tinker. "It will cost you next to nothing."

Now the tinker, who repaired old pots and pans, counted his blessings at having got a new, shiny kettle for such a worthless price. "This is my lucky day!" he said. He tucked the kettle under his arm and went home as happy as he could be.

Sometime during the night, the tinker heard a voice right in his ear: "Tinker! Oh, sir! My good tinker!"

The tinker sat up in his bed. "Who . . . what . . . who's that?" he whispered. Quickly he lit a candle.

Next to his pillow sat the tanuki teakettle with its bushy tail, narrow face, and four tiny feet.

"Why you're the new kettle I got for next to nothing!" said the tinker.

"That I am," said the teakettle. "I'm really a tanuki playing tricks. My name is Bum-bu-ku. And my name means 'good luck'."

"Oh, of course!" cried the tinker, shocked to find a talking tanuki teakettle in his bed.

"You must be quite a poor tinker," said the teakettle, looking around the plain dwelling.

"That I am," the tinker said.

"Well, then, I will help you," said Bumbuku. "But you must promise not to fill me with water and put me over a fire. Treat me kindly—promise—as you would your best friend."

"I promise! You *are* my best friend!" the tinker said, eagerly. "But how can you help me when you are part kettle and part animal?"

"I am a trick tanuki!" said the kettle, wagging its tail. "Build a stage, and I'll be your act. Sell tickets, and we will make a fortune."

"Goodness, that sounds like a fine idea!" said the tinker.

The tinker built a platform for the show. He made a sign that said:

BUMBUKU, THE ONE AND ONLY PRINCE TANUKI TEAKETTLE.

SEE HIM PERFORM HIS MAGIC TRICKS.

All the people flocked to the tinker's theater. They paid the ticket price. And they adored Bumbuku, who could do all sorts of things.

Bumbuku Teakettle danced gracefully. He swayed his long bushy tail in time with his perfect little feet. He sang like a bird, with his narrow face thrust from the teakettle spout. Best of all, Bumbuku walked a high tightrope on his hind legs. One forepaw held a bright fan, which he waved at the audience. The other forepaw raised a red parasol in a princely salute.

"Bumbuku Teakettle, We Love You!" the people cheered.

Each day, the tinker sold many tickets. And every evening after the show, he fed Bumbuku some of the best rice cakes he could find. He was soon a rich man.

"Bumbuku," he said, "I have more than enough money now. And you are tired from working so hard. Would you like to return to the temple of the holy ones and never work again?"

"I wouldn't mind not working," said Bumbuku. "But I don't want to be put back on the fire. I do want to have those tasty rice cakes you give me."

"We shall see about it, then," said the tinker.

The next day, he took Bumbuku Teakettle and his favorite rice cakes to the temple. There, the tinker told the holy man, "Let Bumbuku rest out his days here. Give him these tastiest rice cakes. And *don't* put him on the fire. I'll give you this great amount of money to use as you wish."

Said the holy man: "We will be honored to have the famed Bumbuku stay with us forever. I would not have put him on the fire if I had known about his magic beforehand. Let him have an honored place among us."

So it came to pass that Bumbuku came to stay in a good place. The holy man and his pupils brought a wooden stand to the treasure house and put the teakettle on it. They put rice cakes, the very best, next to the stand.

To this day, there rests Bumbuku, the tanuki magic teakettle, in the temple treasure house. Once in a while, Bumbuku plays a trick and transforms himself into a holy man to fool the pupils. But his bushy tail always gives him away. By this time, all the holy ones know about his tricks.

"I am quite content," Bumbuku is fond of saying. "I have the tastiest rice cakes to eat. And I am never, ever filled with water and put over the fire."

COMMENT

This story of the prankster tanuki is one of many found in Japanese folklore and is a favorite of Japanese children. The tanuki is an animal with a long fuzzy tail and a darkened area around the eyes that resembles the mask of a raccoon. It is sometimes confused with the badger, but in English it is known as a raccoon dog.

The tanuki represents one of the oldest mythological figures. As the trickster, it is the character in folktales who fools others and then is sometimes tricked itself. The trickster is often a transformer, having the ability to change itself into something else.

Fenris, the Wolf

Once there was an evil force, and his name was Loki. He was god of fire, and long ago he went to the forbidden land of the giants. There he married an ugly giantess, who gave birth to three monsters — an evil goddess, a monster serpent, and a mighty wolf child.

Now the great one, Odin, was the high god of the gods. He saw the three monsters and how fast they grew. "When they are stronger," he said, "they might enter the home of the gods and destroy us."

Odin mounted his eight-footed horse and rode through the air to the land of the giants. There he found the first of the three monsters — the evil goddess. Odin flung her down, down into the dark and dank of the land of mists. There she soon reigned over nine worlds and became the queen of the dead.

Next, Odin caught the monster serpent and threw it into the sea. The serpent grew in the ocean until it was able to wrap itself around the earth. It clenched its tail in its mouth, and all humans within the awful circle of it were made prisoners.

Odin was shocked by the size of this beast in the sea. And fearing that the third monster child, the wolf, Fenris, would take over the heavens, he led it to Asgard, the home of the gods. Odin's plan was to have the gods treat Fenris kindly so he would be made gentle.

But the gods were afraid when they saw how huge the wolf was growing. They shrank away and would not feed him. For his jaws and fangs were deadly. But Tiu, son of Odin, had courage. He alone dared come near Fenris. Tiu fed the wolf so well that Fenris grew bigger, stronger, and more fierce each day.

Finally, the gods called a secret meeting to decide how to get rid of the monster wolf. "We cannot kill him here," said one of the gods. "That would bloody our peaceful home."

"Then let us bind him fast," said Odin, "so he can work no harm to us or to humans."

They had a mighty chain made and named it Laiding. They took it out to Fenris's keep. Odin pretended to play with the wolf and said, "We know you are strong, Fenris, but can your great strength burst Laiding?"

"My power is true," growled Fenris. He allowed himself to be bound by the chain. The gods made it fast and tight around him. Eagerly, they stood aside to let Fenris do his best.

The wolf gave a mighty heave. Easily, like shaking off vermin, he broke the chain, Laiding, into pieces.

Oh, how the gods praised his strength! But unknown to Fenris, they had another chain made. Named Droma, the second chain was a hundred times thicker and stronger than the first. Droma would have to be, because now Fenris was so enormous he blotted out the sky.

The gods talked Fenris into letting them bind him with the second chain, Droma. And after a short, hard struggle, he burst that great chain into pieces.

"It is not good," thought Odin. "We need something more." He sent a servant to the land of the dwarfs. "Have them make a bond that is unbreakable," commanded Odin.

The dwarfs fashioned a silk rope. It was made out of six magic strengths: a cat's footsteps, a woman's beard, the roots of a mountain, the longings of the bear, the voice of fish, and the spittle of birds.

"But these things cannot be!" said the servant, when the dwarfs revealed the magic. And yet, being magic, they were indeed. The dwarfs told him the silk bond could not be broken, and the more it was strained against, the stronger its magic would grow.

The gods took the silk bond and again asked Fenris to test his strength. But this time, Fenris did not trust this slender bond. He told the gods, "I will do it if one of you places your hand in my mouth while I am being tied. That will be the proof that there is no trick."

All drew back at these words, except for Tiu. He boldly thrust his hand inside the jaws of monster Fenris. At once, the other gods wound the silk bond around Fenris's body and paws.

Fenris fought mightily against the bonds. Then the gods laughed and shouted, for Fenris could not break away.

In a rage at having been caught, Fenris snapped together his sharp teeth and bit off Tiu's hand at the wrist. The god felt the pain, healed

himself, and lived. But ever after, the wrist has been called the wolf's joint.

Meantime, Fenris struggled while the gods tied the silken bond to a boulder sunk deep into the earth. He howled and howled. To silence him, the gods thrust a sword with the point piercing through the bridge of his mouth and the handle stabbing his lower jaw. His mouth was forced open through days and nights for a long, long time. Blood poured out in streams forming a great river that became known as Von.

"So you will remain," Odin told the wolf.

And so did awful Fenris stay — until the last day of the world.

COMMENT

In Norse mythology, in the Icelandic eddas or "stories," gods are called Aesir, the pillars and supporters of the world. And in the world of Norse myth, there are giants, monsters, men, gods, dwarfs, and elves. Objects such as swords and chains have names and power. Gods come to an end as humans do. And at the twilight of the gods, called Ragnarök (rag-na-ruk), the day of judgment, there is a great battle between Fenris, with his wolf offspring, and his father, Loki, and the gods. Fenris devours Odin, the father of the gods, on the last day of the world. The gods are then struck down. All of the earth sinks beneath the sea. But in a future time, the earth rises once more; it regenerates itself under the sun, and the whole system begins again.

Tiu, son of Odin, was the god of war. To the peoples of the north, he ranked high with Odin. Men cried out to him in praise before going into battle. He became so famous that he was worshiped and had his own special day called Tiu's day — in our modern English, Tuesday.

Joseph Golem

There was a time in Prague, Czechoslovakia, when the Jews there were tormented by their enemies. They were wrongly accused of awful deeds. The most dreadful untruth was that it was their custom to mix the blood of Christian children in the Passover matzo bread they baked. This terrible slander was called the "blood libel."

Still, the Jewish people there did have strong and fearless friends. One was the king himself. He was Rudolf of Bohemia. Another was a great rabbi, Judah Lowe, who was known and respected for his writing and teachings, and for his wisdom. King Rudolf told Rabbi Lowe, "I will not permit the blood accusation to be charged against the Jews of my kingdom."

At once, King Rudolf issued an order. It said that not every Jew had to stand trial in the blood libel. Always before, every Jew would have to stand trial, no matter who was accused. Now, only the *one* person charged would have to go to trial. And that person would never be found guilty unless the charge was proved.

Well, that helped the Jews of Prague, but it did not end their troubles at all. There were still enemies about, some of whom were clever sorcerers. Any one of them who wished to destroy a Jew might take a dead child from its grave and place it in the Jew's house! Yes, the idea is horrible, yet such acts were carried out. And despite King Rudolf's decree, the blood slander against the whole of the Jewish population would begin all over again.

The great and wise Rabbi Lowe called upon God in heaven to help him fight against the enemy. He heard God's voice in a dream. Rabbi Lowe dreamed God said, "Ato Bra Golem Devuk Hachomer V'tigzar Zedim Chevel Torfe Yisroel!" The words seemed to be arranged mysteriously in Hebrew. They meant: "Create a golem, a creature out of clay who will destroy all the enemies of Israel!"

When Rabbi Lowe awakened, he knew there must be magical secrets in the Hebrew words. "I will create this golem of clay, in the shape of a man," he thought. "And I will bring the golem to life as the protector of the Jewish people."

Now Rabbi Lowe understood that in order to make the golem, he would need to bring together the four elements of Fire, Water, Air, and Earth. All of the world and everything in it was made up of these four substances. In fact, people believed lead could be made into gold if one mixed together the right amounts of the four elements.

Rabbi Lowe called upon his son-in-law, Isaac, and his disciple, Jacob, to help him. Isaac had been born mostly of Fire, and Jacob was born of the Water element. Rabbi Lowe had been born of the Air element. The golem, made of clay, was the Earth substance.

The rabbi told Jacob and Isaac his plan. And for seven days, they fasted and prayed to make themselves pure. Before dawn of the eighth day, they went to the river. They took up clay from the river bank and molded the figure of a man ten feet tall. They modeled his head, his face, and his arms and legs, feet and fingers. When they finished, Rabbi Lowe stood with Isaac and Jacob at the golem's feet. The golem of clay lay outstretched on his back.

"Isaac," said the rabbi, "you walk around the thing seven times from right to left." He told Isaac secret charms to say as he walked. Isaac did as he was told. And the golem glowed red as fire.

"Jacob, you must circle around the thing in the other direction from Isaac," said the rabbi.

Jacob did, saying more magic. The golem's fire went out. The clay body filled with water. A cloud of steam rose from it. Then that cleared away. And the golem had grown hair and toenails and fingernails.

Rabbi Lowe took himself around the golem seven times. Next, he bent down and wrote the word emeth, "truth," on the golem's forehead. The word was hardly visible. Only the rabbi could read it.

All three men spoke a passage from Genesis II:7, saying, "The Lord God formed man of the dust of the ground and breathed into his nostrils the breath of life; And man became a living soul." The golem's eyes fluttered open. He stared, confused. At last, he stared in wonder.

It was the second day in the month of Adar (February) in the year 5340 of the Creation (A.D. 1580), that the thing of clay was born.

"Stand up!" Rabbi Lowe commanded the thing.

The golem lumbered up, a monstrous giant of a man. Its arms reached nearly to its knees. Its hands as large as scoops pointed straight to the ground. Its eyes fixed upon its creator.

"Good," spoke the rabbi. And he had the golem dressed in clothes fit for a shammes, an attendant of the synagogue.

"I will call you Joseph," said Rabbi Lowe. "Joseph Golem, you are created to defend the Jewish people against their enemies. You will serve as my attendant in the synagogue. No matter what I tell you, you will obey." The golem stared unblinking at the rabbi. Said Rabbi Lowe, "If I tell you to leap into the fire, Joseph, you will jump high into the flames!"

The golem understood every word, but it could not speak. For God alone gives the power of speech, so they say. Yet the golem could hear quite well. It could recognize sounds from very far away.

Rabbi Lowe wouldn't allow anyone to give the golem work to do. He had not created it for toil. And he told his wife, Pe-re-le, that he had met the poor soul, Joseph, on the street. "I felt sorry for him, so I brought him home," the rabbi said. "Don't bother him with silly tasks. Just let him sit and wait for me to call him."

So, day after day, Joseph Golem sat in a corner of the synagogue all alone. He rested his chin on his hands and looked like an idiot, which all were sure he was. People began calling him Dumb Joseph or Idiot Joseph.

Now Perele soon forgot that Joseph Golem was not to do simple work. One day, she sent him off to market for two baskets of fruit. The fruit woman laughed at the way he looked and how big he was. So Joseph Golem lifted her on his shoulders, with her stand and all of her

baskets of fruit. He went around the city with this load, and everyone laughed and laughed at him.

Another time, Perele sent him for buckets of water to clean the floors. She did not tell him how many buckets she needed. Joseph drew barrels and barrels of water. He caused an awful flood in the house. Someone thought to send for Rabbi Lowe. When he came, he couldn't help laughing. "What a fine waterman you have!" he told his wife. And he led poor Joseph back to his corner.

Well, you can imagine how the incident became the gossip of Prague. All the people whispered about it.

But unknown to the people, or to Perele and the household, Rabbi Lowe was using Joseph Golem to aid the Jews of Prague against many dangers. And with Joseph's help, he was able to stop the blood accusations. When the Rabbi sent the golem on a mission, he made Joseph invisible with a secret word written on a charmed object around the golem's neck. Other times, Rabbi Lowe dressed Joseph like an ordinary porter. Joseph would guard Prague ghetto, the neighborhood of the Jews enclosed by a wall.

"Joseph," the rabbi told him, "walk the streets outside the wall at night, and keep a lookout for those who will do evil to the Jews."

Joseph looked into every wagon passing by and every bundle carried inside the walls. If he suspected anyone, he would tie up the person and take him to the city authority.

Then something awful happened. An enemy owed a rabbi money and didn't want to pay. So this enemy took a newly buried Christian child from the cemetery. He next killed a pig and cleaned out the insides. He cut the throat of the dead child to make it appear that it was murdered. He wrapped the child in a prayer shawl and placed it inside the pig. Much later, he rode to town. And while the rabbi slept, the enemy planned to dump the pig and all in his house.

But when the enemy neared this rabbi's house, he saw a huge monster before him. This was indeed Joseph Golem, ever watchful. Joseph grabbed the pig that held the dead child. He tied up the terrified enemy. He took the man to the courtyard of the authority along with the stuffed pig. Then Joseph hurried away.

The watchmen heard screeching. They swung their lanterns. There lay the enemy tied hand and foot. "Something huge . . . took me and beat me," he stammered. "The monster was dressed like a porter. Oh, he was a giant, a devil!"

The authority could see that the stuffed pig was meant as the blood accusation. No one guessed who the monster was. No one, that is, but our Rabbi Lowe and his helpers. They knew!

Now there was fear among the enemies of the Jewish people. And, slowly, all such enemies fell silent.

Rabbi Lowe met with his son-in-law and his disciple. "We no longer need the golem," he said. "It will be a long time before lies against us are made again."

That very night Rabbi Lowe told Joseph Golem: "Tonight, you will sleep in the attic. Go there!"

Joseph always did as the rabbi commanded him. He went quietly.

After midnight, the rabbi and Isaac and Jacob went up to the attic of the synagogue. They stood there before the sleeping giant golem.

The rabbi shook his head. "Not a monster," he said, "but a creation sent by God to help our people. Now its work is finished. Good-bye, my Joseph!"

The three men took the opposite positions from the way they were when Joseph was created. They stood at his head and gazed down into his face. Together they circled around him, from left to right, turning seven times. They chanted magic words and secret formulas, which have not been repeated since that night.

Rabbi Lowe erased the first letter from the Hebrew word emeth, "truth," on the golem's forehead. What was left was the word meth, or "dead." With that, the light went out of the golem's eyes. Joseph lay stiff and lifeless. He had become a huge, hardened mound of clay.

They wrapped prayer shawls around the golem. Rabbi Lowe and his helpers covered it with pages of old prayer books by the thousands until it was hidden under them. They got rid of Joseph's clothes.

"Never breathe a word of this to anyone," Rabbi Lowe said. "Burn the clothes where no one can see." When this was done they all washed their hands. They said the prayers one speaks after being near a corpse.

In the morning, Rabbi Lowe let it be known that he and Joseph Golem had quarreled. "Joseph has left the city," said the rabbi. Later, Rabbi Lowe forbade anyone to enter the synagogue attic. No one did.

They say the golem still lies in the attic. He is buried there beneath pages from decayed books. Perhaps the golem waits for the coming of the Messiah to give him life. Joseph was a faithful servant, a gentle creation. One day soon, new dangers may threaten the Jewish people, the tribes of Israel. Some say then and only then will Joseph Golem rise again.

So the story is told, and here it ends.

COMMENT

The golem is a figure out of Jewish folklore. The Prague golem was the most popular of all Jewish golem stories and a later version of much older tales. The age-old sorcerer's apprentice motif is a light touch in the scene where Joseph brings water for Perele. Rabbi Judah Lowe of this story was a real person, a renowned religious scholar and philosopher greatly interested in science and the alchemy of his time. His name is also spelled Yehudah Loew or Löw.

The literal meaning of the Hebrew word "golem" is that of lifeless matter. In this story, the golem is brought to life by taking the Hebrew word for truth, "emeth," and writing it on the golem's forehead. Aleph, beth (Alphabet) are the first two letters of the Hebrew alphabet. Aleph is "the beginning." If the beginning, Aleph (that is, the e), is erased from emeth, "truth," there remains the word "meth," meaning "dead." By this magic, the golem was said to die and return to the clay from which it had been formed.

In the Middle Ages and before, people believed in the prescientific four primary substances of earth, air, fire, and water. In a process called transmutation, any substance could be changed into any other by altering the amounts of the four elements. The idea of a creation in the shape of a man is taken directly from Jewish mystical, folkloric sources and is ancient and legendary. It contradicts all rational teachings of Judaism. Nevertheless, Jewish mystics gave the golem the meaning of a living automaton.

Only with the Prague golem story late in the sixteenth century was the monster image given a spark of a soul. The golem then became a God-sent protector and redeemer of persecuted Jews.

The Very Large Son

A woman lived with her very large son in a small cottage on a landowner's grand estate. Not far from the cottage was the great manor house where the landowner lived. The house was the size of a castle, and every hour, the woman would go to the manor house to ask for a pot of buttermilk and a loaf of dark bread.

"Well, then, how many people do you take care of?" the landowner asked the woman one day.

"I have only myself and my son," said the woman.

"Why, the two of you eat as much as ten people," the landowner said angrily. "I want to see this son of yours. Send him here to me."

So the woman went home and told her huge son what the landowner had said.

"What can he want of me?" asked the son. He went quickly to the manor house.

The landowner was waiting. He looked the son up and down. "This lad is a giant!" thought the landowner. And he asked, "What can you do? Can you work?"

"What is that — work?" asked the giant son.

"I'll show you work if you come with me," said the landowner. He took the giant son along and showed him how to pitch cow dung outside the barn.

"Do it like this," said the landowner, and he showed him how.

"That's nothing!" said the giant. He pitched all the dung in one throw.

"What great strength he has!" thought the landowner. "I can use him to do most of my work for free."

"I've a herd of cows across the river," he said. "Lead them through the river to this house. But don't let their hooves get wet."

The giant son took up sacks and a knife. He went across the river and chased the cows. He caught the first one. He chopped off her hooves and put them in a sack. He did the same with all the cows until they were hoofless. Then he herded them across the river and to the castle.

The landowner stood there on the steps. The giant son threw down many sacks, and hooves rolled out at the landowner's feet.

"See, the hooves are not wet," said the giant.

The landowner was furious at what this giant fool had done. Later, he got over his anger. "I want you to do something else for me," he said. "In the field is a lake. Drain it for me."

Off went the giant son. He chopped down a great tree and took it to the lake. He forced the tree under the lake, making a huge hole. He drained all the lake water down into the hole.

The landowner went to see the next morning. The lake was dry. "Where did you get such strength to do that?" he asked the giant.

The giant son wouldn't tell. "I'll show you how strong I am," he said. He took an iron chain and fastened it around the manor house. Next, he dragged that house over beside the cottage where he and his mother lived.

The landowner couldn't believe it. There sat his manor house next to the little cottage.

"I'll give you all my sheep, my cows, and my horses if you tell me where you get your strength," said the landowner.

Well, the giant had nothing to say to this. He had his hand in his pocket, and he drew out the only thing there — a small button. "Take it, take the button," he told the landowner.

The landowner put the button in his pocket. He gave all the animals he owned to the very large son. He thought the button would show him how the giant son got his strength. But three days passed, and he knew nothing more.

"The young man has tricked me," he thought. "I bet he has the devil on his side. I'll go see him and tell him what I think of him."

The landowner went over to the cottage and knocked loudly on the door.

The son opened it.

"You're no better than the devil, you giant!" said the landowner.

"But I *am* the devil, so!" said the giant son, and he knocked the landowner down. That is how the wicked landowner came to be under the devil's hand.

And to this day, the devil son lives in the cottage with his mother.

COMMENT

This is a Welsh gypsy story dating back at least to the seventeenth century. Abram Wood, the King of the Gypsies, told it. It has been told ever since.

This story can be thought of as a cautionary tale. The warning might be: Do not attempt to get something for nothing. It was wrong for the landlord to make the giant son work for nothing. The moral is: Never fool with a giant, for he may be the devil in disguise!

The Free Spirits, Bouki and Malice

Eh, Cric!

AUDIENCE, READER RESPOND: *Eh, Cric! (Aye, Cree)*

Eh, Crac!

RESPOND: *Eh, Crac! (Aye, Crack)*

There is this one about Bouki (Boo-kee) monkey and a rabbit named Little Malice (Mah-lees). And there was a king then in Haiti.

The king had a lamb that he cared for more than all the money in the world. It was like his child, that lamb, and the king played with it as a father would play with his son. The king combed its wool and named it My Joy.

Now the king kept a good lookout for the rabbit, Little Malice, who liked to trick everyone, even the king. And King was awfully afraid that Little Malice would steal My Joy, his lamb, away.

Eh, Cric!

Eh, Cric!

Eh, Crac!

Eh, Crac!

Well, it is so—Little Malice knew about the king's fat lamby-pie. And Malice wanted to eat My Joy for his supper, for he loved the meat of this young animal best of all. And very quickly then, the king's My Joy ended up in Malice's stewing pot. That rabbit Malice ate it all up, too.

Well, the king knew who the thief was, and he sent his guards after Malice.

Then Malice moved just as swiftly. He went out himself to find that fool monkey, Bouki, who also loved eating well. Little Malice knocked on Bouki's door.

"Ah!" said Bouki.

"Bouki, my friend," said Malice. "King offers a prayer and feast for his lost sheep."

"I didn't know that," said Bouki.

"Yes, well, there will be a songfest, as well," said Malice. "He who sings the best song and wears the finest costume will receive very fine prizes."

"That's good!" said Bouki. "Please, Malice, go buy me the best costume and teach me the best song so I can win the prizes. Here is some money. I'll give you half of all I get from the king."

Malice took the money. Next he got the skin from the stolen lamb, and he made Bouki a fine wool coat.

"Oh, you look good, Bouki," he said, putting the coat on the fool. "Now I'll teach you this song that will be the best, and you will win the prize." Malice taught the song:

"I am the smart Bouki
Who stole My Joy from the king.
Eh, Cric!
The truth is on my back.
Eh, Crac!
I stole My Joy from the king.
I ate that tasty thing!"

"Oh, I like that song very much," said Bouki. And he learned the song quickly. Then Malice took him to the king's palace. Bouki went inside.

Malice hid in the bushes outside. "I don't feel well, I don't want to go in," he told Bouki.

Bouki walked around like a king, himself. He ate and drank everything and listened to everyone talk about the king's loss of his My Joy. He thought he would make the king happy as well as win the prizes with his song. And so he commenced to sing:

"I am the smart Bouki
Who stole My Joy from the king.
Eh, Cric!
The truth is on my back.
Eh, Crac!

I stole My Joy from the king.

I ate that tasty thing!"

"What is that I hear?" cried the king.

"It's me," said Bouki. "Listen to my song:

> I am the smart Bouki
>
> Who stole My Joy from the king.
>
> *Eh, Cric!*
>
> The truth is on my back.
>
> *Eh, Crac!*
>
> I stole My Joy from the king.
>
> I ate that tasty thing!"

"Let me see your back!" shouted the king.

Bouki turned so King could see. The king saw the skin of his favorite, My Joy.

"Guards, grab this thief! Hide him away so he won't ever steal a lamb again."

The guards took Bouki out of the palace. Then Malice went inside and said to the king, "It was I who helped you, sire, so you must give me the prizes."

The king was not a fool. He knew that a snake crawls close to its hole in the ground. "The witch doctors says this deed was done by a smart one," said the king. "But everybody knows Bouki is a fool. Malice, I believe you may have done this bad deed!" And he had his guards chain up Malice.

So it happened that Little Malice and Bouki Monkey ended up in the same prison where they waited to be punished.

"You are bad, Little Malice!" cried Bouki. "You did this to me!"

"Yes, I did," said Malice. "I am very sorry I did. I think of you as my friend even when I trick you, Bouki. Don't worry, I'll get us both out of here!" Malice gave gifts to the guards, and before anyone was the wiser, he and Bouki were free spirits.

"I'll not ever listen to you again, Little Malice," promised Bouki.

"I believe you, my friend," said Malice. He smiled. For he knew a hundred ways to make Bouki Monkey listen.

Eh, Cric!

Eh, Cric!

Eh, Crac!

Eh, Crac!

COMMENT

Malice is a famous Haitian folktale character. Bouqui or Bouki is even more well known. In some stories, Bouki and Malice are relatives, uncle and nephew. Stories about them were brought to Haiti by the first slaves. Malice sometimes has the face of a rabbit, the classic symbol of a trickster in African folklore. In early African American folklore, the clever but weak rabbit is the symbol for the slave. Bouki has the face of a donkey or monkey. In the Dominican Republic, a glutton is called a bouqui, and in French Louisianna, a bouqui is a stupid and selfish person. Friendship between trickster and fool is common in world folklore.

The dramatic introductory formula, "Eh, Cric, Eh, Crac," in which the listener responds the same, is a well-established device in folktales in French-speaking countries such as Haiti.

The Girl Who Was Swallowed by the Earth

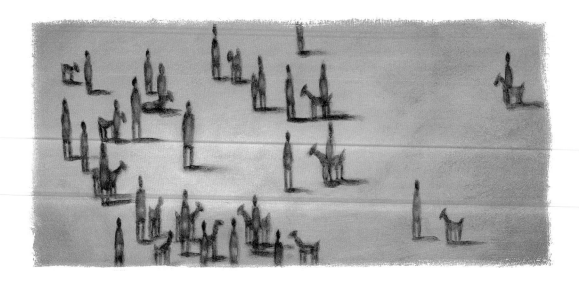

Year after year, it was the same story for the people. The sun glowed red-hot in its bright sky. The rains never came to cool the nights and soften the earth. All of the people's crops died. The people were so hungry they walked like they were very old when they were quite young — when many of them were only children. For three years it was the same story. Burning sun, no rain, and hunger.

Now the people climbed a great hill and gathered at a wide open space on top. And they asked one another, "Why doesn't the rain come?"

One of them thought to answer, "Let's ask the Medicine Man." So they struggled back down the hill, and they said to him, "Tell us what to do. Our crops die, there is no rain. Without water or food we will all perish."

The Medicine Man took up his magic gourd and let its contents fall. He did this again and again until he said to the people, "I see there is a young woman that you must buy if it is to rain. Her name is Wan-ji-ru. Come back here two days from now. Each of you bring a goat to help buy Wanjiru."

So it was that in two days, they all came to stand in a circle, and every man, woman, and child brought a goat. Wanjiru's family stood there with Wanjiru in the center. All at once, her feet sank down into the ground. She sank down to her knees. "Oh, oh!" she cried, "I am lost!"

"We are lost!" her mother and father cried out.

The people came up close and gave their goats to Wanjiru's father and mother. Wanjiru sank down to her waist. "Oh, I am lost!" she cried loudly. "Yet much rain will fall!"

She sank down to her shoulders. But no rain came. Wanjiru said, "Much rain will fall!"

She sank down to her neck.

Suddenly, rain came in a hard downpour. The people brought more goats to her family. The family had to hold the animals and could not let go of them to rescue Wanjiru. She sank down to her eyes. Every time one of her family thought to save her, someone would bring another goat, and the relative would have to take it.

Wanjiru cried in her heart, "My own people have done this. This is the end of me!"

Wanjiru sank under the earth. And the rains came in a complete and heavy downpour that soaked the world, it seemed. The people ran home to their huts to get out of the rain.

A young warrior was in love with Wanjiru. He had heard about what had happened to her. "Wanjiru is lost," he told himself. "Her people have done it. But where has she gone? I'll find out, and I will go there and bring her back."

The warrior took his shield and his spear, and he wandered all over. By nightfall, he came to the place where Wanjiru had gone into the ground. He stood right there, and his feet began to sink just as hers had. He went down and down until the ground covered him. Down under, he found himself on a road. It was the way Wanjiru had gone. And soon he saw her.

Poor Wanjiru was covered in rags. "They gave you up to bring the rain," he told her. "Now the rain has come, and I will take you home again."

The warrior carried Wanjiru to the underground starting place. They rose up to the aboveground and breathed the fresh air of life. Then he took her to his mother's house. There he told his mother, "Don't tell anyone that my Wanjiru has returned. I can't let her go to her own people. They treated her badly."

He and his mother killed goats for Wanjiru to eat. Wanjiru soon grew healthy. The warrior and his mother made goatskin clothing for her to wear. And in no time, Wanjiru looked as lovely as she had before.

One day there was a dance. The warrior went alone, and then his mother and Wanjiru went, after all the people were there. When the relatives saw the young woman they all shouted, "Wanjiru! This is she who was lost!" They ran up to her, but the warrior beat them and kept them back.

"You sold her," he said. "Don't you dare to touch her!"

When the dance was over, Wanjiru went to the mother's house again. And one day, her father and mother and her brothers came there. They felt very bad about what had happened to Wanjiru.

The warrior was not unkind. He gave in to them, saying, "You are her relatives." And he let them greet her and speak with her.

He paid the purchase price for Wanjiru. And he married this one who had been lost. The brave and good warrior and the lovely Wanjiru lived happily ever after.

COMMENT

This is a Kikuyu myth story from Kenya, Africa. It is about death and rebirth or resurrection on course with the cycles of nature. The maid here is sacrificed symbolically to the sun as a vegetation spirit or subgoddess. Obviously, the sun is pleased by the sacrifice and makes the rain fall; thus, the cycle of nature continues. The entire myth can be thought of as a fertility rite of renewal, which will bring the forces of nature and humans into harmony. The strength of family and its importance to the Kikuyu community is made clear. The fact that Wanjiru's family did nothing to save her is not reason enough to keep them from her forever. For, as the warrior says to them, "You are her relatives."

The Witch's Boar

They say that long ago in Italy, witches worked their magic spells and thought up evil. At that time there lived a lord and lady in a palace on the banks of the Arno River. They were so unhappy because they had no children.

One day, the lady gazed from her window upon the green countryside and spied a herdsman taking his pigs to market. Eleven little pink pigs with small, bright eyes and curly tails followed one huge, fat sow.

Unknown to the noble lady, there had been only ten baby pigs when the herdsman started on his way. He never noticed that an extra piggy tagged along.

It was a witch, that eleventh pink pig. She had been creeping and spying under the bridge as the herdsman passed with his herd.

"I'll have a good time!" thought the witch. Eager for adventure, she changed herself into a little pink pig right then and there.

It was just afterwards that the lady caught sight of the herdsman driving the pigs to market. "Oh, to have even a piggy for a baby child!" said the lady. "That would be better than no child."

Just then, the eleventh pig was seen to pause and sniff the wind in the lady's direction. Later, in the night, the witch changed into herself again and flew away to her home, a little house right by a church. There she leaned back in her chair for the rest of the night, whispering and sighing, and making wicked magic and awful spells.

Nine months after this, the noble lady did have a child. The couple rejoiced, but only for a moment. They looked more closely and saw that the newborn was a tiny wild pig, a boar!

The lady cried her heart out and would not be soothed. The lord cringed and trembled in deepest agony. Still, the baby did grow bigger and soon was a fine figure of a boar.

The pig was handsome as boars go, with dark hair and bright eyes. He was graceful and fast on his feet, which was important for a boar. Best of all, he had a quick mind. And soon he began talking just like a human child.

The noble lord and lady grew fond of their wild, four-legged child. They brought wise men to teach him. They covered his tusks and hooves in gold. He had chains of flowers around his neck.

People came from all over to talk to the smart boar. His parents were very proud.

The boar spent a good deal of his time thinking. He looked, seeing all there was to see. He saw that a poor but lovely girl lived next to the palace. Each day, the boar watched her as she walked the path to the

river where she would wash clothes. It was not long before he fell in love with her.

The boar finally told his parents that he wished to marry the young woman. They didn't know what to tell him.

The lord said, "No matter that our son is so wonderful; we can't ask the poor maiden to marry a wild boar!"

"Even though she has no dowry," agreed the lady, "we cannot ask that of her."

The wild son was very sad and longed for his love. His hooves and tusks no longer gleamed. His shiny eyes faded, and his head hung down to the ground.

The young woman could well see what was happening to the princely boar. She knew that each day he watched her from his balcony. And she had grown to love him.

"I want to marry him," she said, simply. "He is a fine boar, and if he will have me, I will have him."

All of her family and friends were against the marriage of boar and poor maid. All tried to change her mind.

"No," said the young woman, "the great boar needs me."

The boar was overjoyed. Soon the two were married. The boar's parents did everything for the bride. They gave her jewels and lace for wedding presents. One floor of the palace was set aside for the newly wed couple.

That night, who should enter the bride's chambers? Not a great boar at all, but the most handsome and noblest of young noblemen. "I am truly your bridegroom," said the young man, who had been the boar.

His bride was shocked. "I . . . don't understand," she stammered.

"The wicked witch changed me into a boar," said the groom. "Because you loved me as a boar enough to marry me, part of the spell is broken. The witch must let me be myself from sunset to sunrise."

"Oh, lovely! Oh, I am pleased," said the bride. "You are my prince!"

"But you mustn't tell a soul," said the groom. "If you do, the witch will make me a boar forever. Do you understand?"

"I do!" said the bride. "I won't breathe a word of this to anyone."

Yet she couldn't help telling her mother the secret. After all, she mustn't keep such news from her own dear mother. "Don't you tell a soul!" she warned her mother.

"I wouldn't dare," swore the mother. But she couldn't help telling her friend, who told the priest; and he was overheard by — well, so it went. The secret was soon the town gossip.

When the bride saw her prince again, his gaze upon her was deeply sad. "You did not keep our secret," he said, taking her in his arms. "I will be a boar forever. And as for you, my love, who talked too much, the witch will make you a frog who says the same thing, over and over again."

"Oh, no! Please, no!" cried the young woman.

"Oh, yes," said the boar. "I will see you when I go for a drink at the spring near the river. But the two of us will be husband and wife no longer, from this moment on."

All at once, he was a boar again. His hooves clicked on the marble floors as he left the palace for the last time. Then the witch changed the maiden into a frog.

Years went by. The boar drank at the spring each day. He talked to the green frog sitting there:

> "I am here, little frog!
> He who once you held so dear.
> We two are ever parted,
> Not by evil or by wrong,
> But 'cause you could not hold
> your tongue!"

"Oh, sadness, forgive me, please — rib-bot, rib-bot — sadness, forgive me," cried the little green frog. "Rib-bot, rib-bot, rib-bot . . ."

So says the frog to this day, and evermore.

COMMENT

This legend from Italy is quite old and has a double transformation motif within the beauty-and-the-beast theme. The prince becomes a boar, and the princess becomes a frog. The witch, having accomplished her powerful dirty work, disappears from the action.

The story is part fable and part cautionary tale. The young woman, although good and kind, makes a terrible mistake. Because she talked too much, she brought disaster to herself and to the prince.

The Argument

Poor families are known in this country. And it is not uncommon for the children of the poor to do well in school and better themselves. But they tell here of a special boy who — though poor — was rich in knowledge and cleverness.

He learned everything quickly; his family saved enough money so that he could become a priest. He did become a fine priest, too. There was not another one like him in the whole land, for he could argue better than anyone, and it was therefore thought that he knew more than the bishops.

At this time, the priests taught the people. And since this man, once poor, was the smartest in the country, all the kings of foreign lands sent their sons to him. Oh, and the priest grew proud — how could he not? He even forgot where he'd come from. He forgot his poor mother and father. He forgot about God, who had caused him to be the priest and man that he was. He became so proud that soon he was arguing that he could prove there was no purgatory or no heaven! And then he said, "There is no hell!"

Finally, the priest's argument brought him to the thought that human beings had no souls. "They are like cows and horses or even dogs," he said. "And when they die, that is all there is."

Well, how could anyone disprove him? So they came to believe that all he said was true. Word got around that there was no afterworld. So everyone thought they might as well do whatever they liked in this one. Even kings and kings' sons believed the priest's words. His beliefs were spread far and wide in many lands.

Then, one night, a glowing angel came out from heaven, it did, and it came down to the priest's house. The angel told the priest, "You have only twenty-four hours to live."

Oh, the priest did tremble at that! "Please, please!" he said. "Let me stay a little longer."

The angel stared coldly at him. "Why should you have a longer time? You are a sinner, are you not?"

"But, sir, have pity on my soul," pleaded the priest.

"Oh, so now you have a soul," the angel said. "When did you learn that?"

"I have felt it here in my chest since you came into my house," said the priest.

"What good was all your knowledge if it couldn't convince you that you had a soul until now?" asked the angel.

"No good at all, my lord," sobbed the priest. "And now I know I am to die, but how soon may I enter into heaven?"

"You? In heaven? Never," said the angel. "You said there was no heaven."

"Then shall I go to purgatory?" the priest asked.

"But you said there was no purgatory, either. You will have to go straight to hell," said the angel.

"But, sir, I said there was no hell, too, so I can't be sent there."

The angel now had to stop and think. "Well," he said at last, "here is what can be done for you. You can live now on earth for a hundred years more, having your pleasure as you wish and then be cast to hell for eternity. Or you may die in twenty-four hours in awful torment, and go to purgatory. You will stay there until Judgment Day — that is, if you will find one person who believes. Through that person's faith, you will then be given mercy, and your soul will be saved."

"Then I will die in twenty-four hours," said the priest, "and my soul will be saved."

The angel left all in a glowing, the way he had come.

The priest went back to the royal scholars who awaited his words. He stood full of fear but managed to say, "Pupils, I taught you lies. There is a God, and all beings have immortal souls. Now I believe all that I once said I didn't." But the scholars would not let him finish.

They shouted with laughter. "Master, lord, prove it. Prove it. Have you seen God? Have you seen a man's soul?"

The priest had no answer other than what he cried to them. "There is a God! I know there is!"

They laughed at him. "Show him to us. Let him show himself!" The priest ran from them. Everywhere he went men said, "We believe all you taught us. There is no God, no soul, no purgatory, no heaven, and no hell. Father, you have taught us well."

The priest found a place to be alone, and he moaned with fear, for soon he was to die. But then a boy came his way. "God save you," said the boy.

The priest lifted himself to see who had spoken. "And you believe in God?" he asked the boy.

"I've come to learn about him," said the boy.

"The best school and teacher are near here," the priest told him, meaning his school and himself.

"Oh, not that place or that man," said the boy. "I'm told he says there is no God, no heaven nor hell, either. He says men have no souls because he can't see the souls."

"What would you say to that man?" asked the priest.

"I'd ask him to show me his life," said the boy.

"But he couldn't do that," the priest said. "Life can't be seen; we have it, but it is not visible to us."

"Then we *can* have souls, although we can't see them," said the boy.

With that, the priest began to cry from happiness, for he had found a true believer as the angel said he must if his soul was to be saved.

"I want you to take my knife," the priest said to the child. "Stab me until I die. Then watch me, for a thing will rise out of me, and that is my soul rising to God. And when you see it, boy, quickly call the scholars so they may see that my soul has left me. They will see there is a God who punishes; there is a heaven and a hell. . . ."

The child prayed to have strength to do the deed. Then he rose and struck the priest's heart with the knife. But the priest couldn't die until

his twenty-four hours were over. At last, his pain and agony ended. The still hand of death rested on his mouth and eyes. The boy watched, transfixed, as a living thing with snow-white wings began to rise from the body and flutter around him.

The boy ran to get the scholars. When they came they knew they were seeing the soul of their teacher. They watched in awe as the soul passed among the clouds.

All say this was the first butterfly ever seen in that land. And now we all know that butterflies are souls of the once living. They wait for the time they may go into purgatory where they will pass through to purity and peace — or not.

COMMENT

This is an ancient Irish legend of resurrection, having some basis in the version of the resurrection of Christ as told in the Gospel of John. In the Christian tradition there is the belief in a Last Judgment and in the soul, which rises after a person dies. This tale ends with the butterfly rising as the soul of the priest. It is also the first butterfly ever seen in Ireland. The assumption is that this is the first butterfly ever; thus the legend is part pourquoi story, telling how the butterfly came to be.

In Roman Catholic doctrine, purgatory is the place or condition of the soul of a person dying repentant. The soul has not been purified from the stain of pardonable offenses against God. Souls in this condition or state must be purged before entering heaven. Moreover, they can be helped by the faithful on earth. So it is that the priest of our story can be saved from hell by the boy who has faith. But, as the angel says, the priest must remain in purgatory until Judgment Day when he and all others will be judged by their deeds on earth.

The Magician's Fellow

There was a young fellow who was not very smart, but he was both pupil and servant to a great man. The man was well known and very wise. He knew languages, and he knew magic mysteries about the creation of the world.

In the man's house was a chamber room full of wonders beyond belief. There were glass beakers and bottles for changing copper to gold and lead into silver. A large shell, when held to the ear, let the great man listen in on the conversation of anyone he wished to know. And there was a wall mirror in the chamber in a gold and silver frame. Through this mirror the great man was able to see all that went on in the world.

But the most wonderful object in the room was an enormous book. It was covered in black leather. The clasp had been cast from iron, and the corners of the book were made of iron as well. This huge book told all the secrets of the spirit world beyond.

Now, the great man kept his dark, heavy book chained to a table; the table was clamped by iron bands to the floor. No one but this man ever read from the book. And in order to read from it, he had to unlock it with an iron key.

"You will leave the chamber when I enter it. Never are you to go near the black book," the great man told his good fellow. "Enter the room where it is kept only when you need to put the room in order."

So the fellow did as he was told — most of the time. Once in a while, he could not help studying the great man from the shadowy hall as the gentleman pored over his book and read it out loud. The young servant learned many things about the book.

It told the number of angels in heaven. It told that angels sang in choirs, and what kind of work they did and what powers they had. It even told the names of demons and how they could be called upon to do certain tasks.

The great man was out of the house one day when curiosity overcame the young fellow. He entered the chamber of the black book and took his time looking all around.

Since he lived in the great house with the great man, surely, he thought, he and the great man were much the same. No doubt he was as smart as the great man.

So the young pupil thought he would do as he had seen the gentleman do. He took up a bottle and mixed the elements in it. But hard as he tried, he could not turn copper into gold, nor lead into silver. He stared into the framed mirror, but all he saw there were dark clouds and gray smoke. He held the large shell to his ear and heard only the sound of oceans and waves breaking and crashing upon rocky shores.

"I can't do it right!" he cried. "Oh, if I only knew the proper words. But they are all locked inside the black book."

Then he walked near the forbidden book and—good heavens! The fellow was shocked beyond belief, for the black book lay with its clasp open. "The great man has forgotten to lock it with his key!" he cried.

He leaned on the table and slowly and carefully opened the huge book. The pages were written in black and red ink. He understood very little of it. Yet, with his fingers pressed under the words, he was able to spell and murmur a line or two out loud.

Suddenly, all went black around him. A deafening roll of thunder caused the house to shudder. There before him stood an awful, ugly thing. It was a wretched and horrible thing. Its breath went in and out in streams of fire. Its eyes lit up like flaming lamps. It was a demon. The fellow had spoken its name from the black book just a moment before.

And there stood Be-el-ze-bub, the fallen angel. He was the chief devil—old Satan, himself.

"You called me; therefore, I am chained to you," said old Beelzebub. "What do you wish done?"

The poor pupil was too terrified to speak. He could only gasp and tremble from head to foot.

"Tell me what you wish!" said Beelzebub. "If you won't, I will choke the life out of you!"

And with that, the devil grabbed the boy by the throat and burned him with his clawish hands.

"Oh! Oh!" gasped the young fellow. "Water . . . yes! Pour water on that flower there!"

He pointed at a pretty flower on the floor. The great man was fond of it and had the young fellow care for it each week.

The devil disappeared in an instant. In another instant, he was back with a huge barrel of water. He poured the whole thing over the flower. He left and came back with another barrel; he poured that over the flower, too. And this he did, on and on, until the floor was deep in water.

The water was rising. It passed the young fellow's knees and on. It rose to his waist. Old Beelzebub kept the barrels coming. The water climbed to the foolish servant's shoulders, and he jumped up on the table, atop the black book.

The water rose to the windows; it swirled around the fellow's legs. It picked up bottles and the pretty flower and swirled them as well.

"Stop it! Stop it, please, oh, spirit!" cried the pupil. But Beelzebub went at his task as if he'd never stop. And he wouldn't have, either. He would have drowned the whole world, in time, if the great man had not remembered that he had forgotten to lock his black book with the key. He hurried home just as his poor pupil was about to swallow mouthfuls of water.

The great man ran to his chamber. He swam to the book, to Beelzebub, and said the magic words that only he knew.

At once, awful Beelzebub sank back to his hellish, fiery realm below, and the water swept out of every door and window.

Well, the great man was also a kind man. "You are my pupil," he said to the young fellow. "I think this has been a good lesson for you."

And so it was.

COMMENT

This is a version of the age-old and worldwide story of the magician's or sorcerer's apprentice who gets into trouble when hearing only some of the magician's magic words. He foolishly repeats them, to his considerable discomfort. The famous motif of calling up the devil to have him work without being able to get him to stop is considered comical and cautionary in every instance. In one version, a wizard's son reads from the forbidden book, causing flowers to sing and birds to dance. In another version, a lizard magician is keeper of a sword. A tricky rabbit overhears enough magic to command the sword to cut down all of the lizard's corn. But he does not learn the reverse words to stop the sword from cutting everything else in sight.

Brothers and Bone

Once, not too long ago, a wild hog came into our king's country. It killed cattle, and it killed anybody in its path. King said he would give a reward to anyone who got rid of the beast. But the hog was so huge and mighty, so awful to look upon, that no one dared go near the forest where it roamed.

Finally, two brothers said they would do it, rid the country of the hog. The oldest brother was tough and clever; call him John. The youngest was kind and trusting; call him Little Tom. When it came time for them to kneel before our king, he told them: "Go into the forest. Little Tom, you shall stand at one end, and John, you at the other. That way your chances are better for trapping the wild hog."

So John started at the west end of the forest. Little Tom started at the east. Soon after the young one entered, he came upon a very small man, a dwarf, who carried a black spear.

"I give you my spear," said the dwarf. "Your heart is good and pure. Attack the beast with this, and you will not be harmed."

Little Tom thanked the dwarf. Taking the spear, he went bravely on his way. It wasn't long before the swine crossed his path. The huge hog attacked. Little Tom had no time even to holler out. He raised the spear. The hog lunged, and the spear pierced its heart. The great hog died even while its legs kept moving.

Little Tom took the dead hog upon his back and struggled toward home with it. Once out of the forest, he passed an inn where there was merrymaking and laughter. Brother John had gone there to get up his courage with drink. When he saw that Little Tom had already caught the wild beast, why, he turned red with anger and jealousy.

Yet John hid his feelings and called to Little Tom, "Come in, dear brother, have a drink!"

Little Tom gladly went in, for he was tired from his heavy load.

"I'll carry it for you," said John. "But first, let's make merry!"

The brothers had a good time. Little Tom told all about the dwarf who gave him the black spear. He told how he had killed the wild hog. Little Tom stayed late at the inn, and he and John left together.

On the way home, as they crossed the town bridge, they walked one behind the other. Little Tom was in the lead. John brought up the rear, carrying the dead hog as he had said he would. But halfway across, John dropped the hog and leaped on his brother. He clubbed Little Tom. John had hidden a heavy mallet there on the bridge, and that is what he used to beat his brother.

Little Tom fell down dead. John buried him in the ground near the water beneath the bridge, and he took away the wild hog.

John told King he had killed the beast. "The wild hog surely gored my dear brother to death and ate him before I killed it," said John. He looked so sad.

All believed him. And that was how he was given King's daughter in marriage.

Years went by. One time, a herdsman brought his sheep across the bridge. There on the ground close to the water beneath the bridge, he happened to see a bone. It was not so large, but it shone there like a piece of the moon. That was how he was able to see it, it shimmered so in the light.

"What a fine mouthpiece this bone will make for my horn!" exclaimed the shepherd. He got the bone and, later, he carved out a mouthpiece to fit his horn. The first time he blew it, the bone started singing all by itself:

> "Friend, shepherd, you blow upon my bone,
>   My very own!
>   Brother John clubbed me from behind;
>   Then buried me beside the water.
>   He stole the beast I speared myself,
>   And married King's daughter!"

"Oh, it's a wonderful horn I have!" cried the herdsman. "It sings on its own. I shall take it and show it to King."

King heard the horn. This great lord knew what the singing bone mouthpiece meant to tell him. And he had the ground dug up below the bridge. There lay the rest of the bones of Little Tom.

That is how brother John was caught by his own wickedness. Of course, he was punished, and rightly so. King had him sewn in a sack and thrown in the water — under the bridge! And slowly, ever so slowly, bad John drowned and sank to the bottom.

There is a splendid tomb in the churchyard. King had it built. And there Little Tom has lain, from the time not too long ago clear to now.

COMMENT

The idea of the life sign or soul double can be found in folk stories from Germany to Africa. The double or sign may reside in some part of the body — a bone or a skull — or in a thing — a stump, a box, or a tree. When the life sign talks or sings, it tells us whether the person or animal is well, or in danger, or sick. There are tales of the singing bell, drum, crow, goose, and tortoise, and of the talking boat, fish, house, nightingale, pot, and stone. The tale is also one with a reward and punishment motif. John is punished by the king for his terrible deed. Little Tom, who is good, is given a grand tomb as his final resting place.

Yama, the God of Death

Yama, the God of Death, ruled over the kingdom of Yamapur in the underworld. His skin was green, and his fiery red eyes matched the flowing red garments he wore. Yama rode on a buffalo, with a noose in one hand and a spiked metal club in the other. He caught his victims with the noose; if they tried to escape, he threatened them with his club.

God Yama had many messengers. Two of them were thirsty four-eyed dogs. Their black nostrils gushed smoke as they guarded the road to Yamapur. Sometimes the dogs wandered the world for Yama, doing whatever he commanded. Yama also sent the crow and the pigeon, to announce someone's death. The dogs were right there, then, ready to carry the dead one's soul back to Yamapur.

Each black day in Yamapur the god in his dark palace sat on his judgment throne. There he listened to the confessions of the newcomers. And these were the souls of the dead.

Next to the throne was a massive judgment book. Yama's secretary read out loud everything a dead one had done when it was alive. Afterwards, Yama decided the fate of the soul. If the soul had belonged to a good person, it might go to one of the heavens—Pitris or Svarg. The soul would find happiness before coming back to the world again. For it was believed that a soul would be reborn in a new body. But if the soul had been someone evil in life, then it would go to one of the twenty-one hells. Which hell that would be depended on how awful its bad deeds were.

The other gods stayed away from Yama because he brought such sorrow to those who were alive. Yet Yama had many wives. One was a mortal woman he married while pretending he was human. She never knew who he really was.

She and Yama had a son who they named Yama-Kumar. As time passed the wife grew moody, sullen, and quite mean. She and Yama could never agree how Yama-Kumar should be raised. She shouted that Yama-Kumar should be allowed to do exactly as he wished and given what he wanted when he cried. Yama argued that such treatment would only make the boy demanding and impossible to live with. They fought, and they fought.

Finally, Yama could take it no more. "Do whatever you wish with him," he told his wife. "I'm tired of your bad temper!"

Yama left and went home to Yamapur. Being a god, he could watch his son from his castle. And, sadly, he watched his son grow spoiled and unable to care for himself.

One night, Yama decided to visit Yama-Kumar. He appeared before the boy in his room. "My son," said Yama, "I will give you the gift of

healing if you will learn to use the proper herbs and plants. You must learn to work very hard."

"Oh, I will, my father. Thank you!" said Yama-Kumar, very pleased. He had grown bored with having everything given to him.

Yama-Kumar soon did everything well. He learned quickly, and in another year, he became a doctor.

Yama was so proud of him. "Listen well, my son," he said, on another secret visit to his son's room. "Every time you stand at the bedside of someone sick, I will tell you a truth. If the patient can get well, I will nod. But when the patient cannot get well, I will shake my head. Then you must not treat that patient."

"As you wish, my father," said Yama-Kumar. The young doctor became well known for his fine treatments and cures.

Not many years later, a princess became ill. Doctors were called, but none could make her well. The princess was weak and no more than skin and bones when Yama-Kumar was finally called upon.

He came to the princess's bedside. At once God Yama appeared. He shook his head from side to side. This meant the princess must die.

"No, Father!" pleaded Yama-Kumar. "She is beautiful and so young. Let her live a while longer with her family. They love her so."

Growling, Yama said, "She has three days. I give her that much because of you, my son, and your goodness. But warn her loved ones that she has only *three more days*."

Yama-Kumar thanked his father and told the parents the truth. "Yet I believe if she can hold on, your daughter will live for a century," said Yama-Kumar.

He sat down by the young woman to help her live. Three days later, God Yama appeared at the bedside. He would now take the princess to his dark and deadly kingdom.

"Father," said Yama-Kumar, "if you try to take her away before she is a century old, I'll tell Mother who you *really* are and where she can find you!"

God Yama nearly fell over at the mention of his mortal wife. He began to shake all over. "Please, no! Don't tell your mother where to find me. If I have to live with that woman, I'll die myself of her spitting tongue and her fussing!"

Then he calmed down. He saw his son smiling, and Yama smiled back. "You are a smart one, my son," he said. "And because you are, I will allow the princess to live."

Yama went away, and the princess revived. A week later, Yama-Kumar told the royal parents that their daughter was cured.

The king and queen were overjoyed. "You may marry our daughter!" they told Yama-Kumar. And so he did. He, the son of Death and a mortal woman, married the lovely princess.

They say the two of them lived happily for a hundred years.

COMMENT

In the mythology of India, Yama is the god of death, and the son of Surya, the great sun god. Because Surya's wife, Sanjna, could not stand Surya's heat, he cursed her. And he banished her son, Yama, to the underworld. All those above would despise him for bringing misery to humans.

Yama's twin sister, Yamini, was made to live in the form of a wayward river because she was fickle like her mother.

The three other old gods of India are Indra who controls the atmosphere and rain; Vritra, the drought demon god; and Agni, god of fire, who rides a ram.

Yama is sometimes described as the first who died. The resting place of the dead, which he presides over, is located in the south under the earth.

Yama can be found in Buddhist mythology in China, Tibet, and Japan. However, he occupies a lesser position as merely guardian of the home of the dead.

Note that the story makes passing mention of the rebirth of the soul. This is called reincarnation, the belief that when one dies, one's soul or spirit comes back to earth in another body or form. The good soul finds happiness in heaven before being reborn into another life.

The Witch's Skinny
by Virginia Hamilton

Oh, witches live, yes!

Watch out for owls. Watch out for cats and frogs or a large beetle or a cockroach. Take a fork and jam it into the thing, cat or frog, beetle or cockroach. Sure enough, there'll be a witch, sheself. A witch can look just like a shadda — a spirit — sometimes.

Now you know Big Henry? Well, a cat come falling out of the sassafrass tree on him. And it wouldn't let go. It stay right there on Big Henry's back. And though he big, Henry couldn't shake off that black cat. It rode him all day, no matter how hard he ran. When Big Henry ran scared, it looked like the man grew even bigger.

We all us were there under the trees, working the fields. And here come Big Henry just dragging heself. The cat be gone but we know it been on Henry's back. For the claw marks of the cat went most through his shirt and his blood dried out from the slashes. And Big Henry, once always jolly, be down and out all in heself. And there was this mark in the corner of his mouth where that cat witch has put her bridle bit for to ride him. Then Big Henry got way sick, and he said his feet tingled him.

That night, the witch came back — like a dark shadda floated in on him. Came in the window and folks seen her and say, "There come the witch after poor Big Henry."

And the next day, they went in there and Henry's hair on his head all braided up into little stirrups so that cat witch could ride him. His face all scratched up, too.

This happened to Big Henry for 'bout one, two months. He still tall but he got lean and leaner till he was so lean, he weren't Big Henry most at all. He was half-dead, stone-scared Henry. He was dying slowly Henry. And wild-eyed, moaning, and crying Henry. And no folks want to visit him. All his chil'ren left him. His wife was so scared she went running home to she mama, too. But she mama said, "You go on back home, I'll be coming directly."

See, Big Henry's wife's mama was a two-head. She could see both front and back of her — she could read the future, the past, or anybody, even any witch.

"I know how to save Big Henry," she said. "Don't know why folks haven't called on me sooner."

So she hurried over to Big Henry's house. He was lying up all in the bed. He more than half dead now. And panting, can't move. Just help-less. And right before big Mama got to there, the witch came in. Witch had no idea that a two-head was on the way.

Well, it was getting dark out and the witch was ready for her night ride. She going to take Big Henry up in the air. And she weren't hurrying herself at all. But lo and behold, she done what she shouldn't never done but what we hear tell witches will do. None of us has seen it. But she done it. That witch woman got real bold. Never bothered to turn herself into some black cat witch. No! But came on in there; she saw Big Henry couldn't move, lying with he face to the wall.

So she took off her skin, that witch did! Oh, yes she did, too! And hung it up there beside big Henry's work-alls. I say she hung up she skin, for true. And she shadda take hold of Big Henry. Put the bit in his mouth and stirrup his hair on his head.

And now Big Henry looking most like a horse. But he weren't no horse. He be poor Henry, the witch's ride. She rode right out the window. Folks saw 'em climbing up the night breeze toward the moon. Oh, it was an awful sight, some say. And poor Henry was a-whinnying like he about to die.

And then big Mama come in there. Looked all around. Folks brave enough to come in behind her. "They gone," folks telling Mama. "You too late."

"Too late, nothing," big Mama said. She took out her red-pepper box. It was all oily and peppery, too. And she sprinkled that oil-pepper into the witch's skin. "Now let's *move*," big Mama said. And they all got outta there in a hurry, for the witch be coming back very soon. Witches never ride somebody for too long.

So the witch brought poor Big Henry on back after she ride. She stretched him face down on the bed. She screeched at him, said she'll be back next night, too. Then the witch went for her skin. She took it down and tried to slip it on. The skin felt funny when she got it on. She talked to it.

"Skin?" she said. "Don't you feel all right? Skinny, what the matter, you? Don't you know who it be inside you? It's me, big Witch!"

That skin usually talked a mile a minute, but this time it can't say a thing, it so tight in. The witch started moaning. She started crying out loud and hopping all around and up and down. "Skinny! Don't you know me? Don't you know me, Skinny!" the witch hollered.

But Skinny so hot and hurt and stung so that it squeezed up the witch until it squeezed her breath out. She 'came stone dead, too. I wouldn't lie to you, either.

So that's how Big Henry got free of the witch woman cat. After the witch be dead — they found cat fur all over the place and scraps of skin on the floor at the foot of Big Henry's bed — big Mama came in and sprinkled some salt and pepper around the room. Witches hate them so bad, too. And that scrap skin shriveled up and disappeared. Mama put a broom in the doorway. You know, no witch is going to jump over a broom!

"Don't you worry, Big Henry," Mama said. "I'll make you soup today and greens tomorrow. You'll be fine in no time."

And so he was, too. Big Henry rested up and pretty soon, he all healed up. His wife and chil'ren came back home. In a week more, he went on back to work. He be a nice man, just like always. But one thing about him. When he go by a sassafrass tree, he makes a wide circle. He won't walk under it, ever. And he slaps his hands along his back, to make sure nothing catch hold it. That's how everybody know it be Big Henry going by. For true.

COMMENT

This story is told with a light touch of colloquial speech to depict a folk character with intimate knowledge of events. The extraordinary number of witch beliefs in black folklore gave the author the opportunity to combine witch descriptions and create the characters of Big Henry, the witch, Mama, the folks, and the narrator to form a tale that would faithfully display a variety of omens and beliefs. The lore of the witch hanging up her skin is widespread in America and Africa as well as the Bahamas. Witches ride people in daylight and at night, for people riding is the chief witch activity. Braiding a horse's mane or a person's hair simply invites a witch to ride.

Whether tellers of witch lore actually believed in witches is anybody's guess. But we can assume that often the stories were told in the same manner in which ghost stories were told—both to scare the listener and have the listener be the judge.

Other lore has witches living in stumps and hollow logs and in caves. Witches can change into gnats or horses, buzzards, cats, beetles, and almost anything. A witch will not step over a broom. And forks, salt, and pepper are important in stopping witch activity. The witch's spirit can project and transform itself. But harm can be brought to the spirit by treating the witch skin in the proper manner. A final capture method is this: trap a witch in a bottle that has been "spelled" (a spell has been put on the bottle). By placing the bottle in the hot ashes of a fire, the witch will suffer greatly and die.

USEFUL SOURCES

Addiss, Stephen, ed. *Japanese Ghosts & Demons: Art of the Supernatural.* New
     York: George Braziller, 1985.

Aldington, Richard and Delano Ames, trans. *New Larousse Encyclopedia of
     Mythology.* Buffalo, N.Y.: Prometheus Press; London: Hamlyn Publishing
     Group, 1968.

Alexander, Hartley B. *North American Mythology.* Vol. 10 of *The Mythology of
     All Races.* 1916. Reprint. Cambridge, Mass.: Archaeological Institute
     of America, 1936.

Anesaki, Masaharu. *Japanese.* Vol. VIII of *The Mythology of All Races, in Thirteen
     Volumes.* New York: Cooper Square Publishers, 1964.

Ausubel, Nathan, ed. *A Treasury of Jewish Folklore.* New York: Crown Publishers,
     1948.

Baker, Margaret. *Folklore of the Sea.* London: Newton Abbot; North Pomfret, Vt.: David & Charles, 1979.

Beck, Horace. *Folklore and the Sea.* Middletown, Conn.: Wesleyan University Press in association with the Marine Historical Association, 1973.

Ben-Asher, Naomi and Hayim Leaf, eds. *The Junior Jewish Encyclopedia.* rev. ed. New York: Shengold Publishers, 1970.

Bierhorst, John. *The Mythology of North America.* New York: William Morrow & Co., Quill Trade Paperbacks, 1985.

Briggs, Katharine M., comp. *Folk Legends.* Vol. I of *A Dictionary of British Folk-Tales—Part B.* Bloomington: Indiana University Press, 1971.

Bulfinch, Thomas. *The Golden Age of Myth and Legend.* London: Branken Books, 1985.

Campbell, Joseph. *Myths to Live By.* 1972. Reprint. New York: Bantam Books, 1973.

————. *The Masks of God: Oriental Mythology.* 1962. Reprint. New York: Penguin Books, 1976.

————. *The Masks of God: Primitive Mythology.* 1959. Reprint. New York: Penguin Books, 1976.

Carpenter, Frances. *Tales of a Chinese Grandmother.* Garden City, N.Y.: Doubleday, 1937.

Caso, Alfonso. *The Aztecs.* Translated by Lowell Dunham. Norman, Okla.: University of Oklahoma Press, 1958.

Chinese Myths. Shanghai, China: Juvenile and Children's Publishing House, n.d.

Christie, Anthony. *Chinese Mythology.* London: Hamlyn Publishing Group, 1968.

Croker, Thomas Crofton. *Fairy Legends and Traditions of the South of Ireland.* 3 vols. 1825–28. Reprint (3 vols. in 1). New York: Lemma Publishing Corp., 1971.

Davis, Mary Gould. *The Truce of the Wolf and Other Tales of Old Italy.* New York: Harcourt, Brace and Co., 1931.

Dolch, Edward W. and Margurite. *Stories from Old Russia.* Champaign, Ill.: Garrard, 1962.

Eliade, Mircea. *Shamanism: Archaic Techniques of Ecstasy.* Translated from French by Willard R. Trask. Bollingen Series LXXVI. New York: Pantheon Books, 1964.

Emerson, Ellen Russell. *Indian Myths.* (alternate title *Legends, Traditions and Symbols of the Aborigines of America).* Boston: James H. Osgood & Co., 1884.

English Fairy Tales. Retold by Flora A. W. Steel. New York: Macmillan, 1918.

Ferguson, John C. *Chinese.* Vol. VIII of *The Mythology of All Races, in Thirteen Volumes.* New York: Cooper Square Publishers, 1964.

Folk Tales and Fables of the World. Retold by Barbara Hayes. New York: Portland House, 1987.

Foster, James R., ed. *The World's Great Folktales.* New York: Harper & Brothers, 1953.

Gaster, Moses, trans. *Ma'aseh Book: Book of Jewish Tales and Legends,* 2 vols. 1934. Reprint (2 vols. in 1). Philadelphia: Jewish Publication Society of America, 1981.

Georgia Writers' Project, Savannah Unit. *Drums and Shadows: Survival Studies Among the Georgia Coastal Negroes.* 1940. Reprint. Westport, Conn.: Greenwood Press, Publishers, 1973.

Grimms' Tales for Young and Old: The Complete Stories. Translated by Ralph Manheim. Garden City, N.Y.: Doubleday, Anchor Press, 1977.

Guerber, H. A. *The Norsemen: Myths & Legends.* New York: Avenel Books, 1985; distributed by Crown Publishers.

von Hagen, Victor Wolfgang. *The Ancient Sun Kingdoms of the Americas.* New York: World Publishing Company, 1961.

Hamilton, Edith. *Mythology.* New York: A Mentor Book, NAL, 1969.

Harn, Lafcadio, and others. *Japanese Fairy Tales.* New York: Liveright Publishing Corporation, 1953.

Harris, Joel Chandler. *Uncle Remus: His Songs and His Sayings.* Boston: Houghton Mifflin Company, 1880.

Haviland, Virginia. *Favorite Fairy Tales Told in Russia.* Boston: Little, Brown & Co., 1961.

Henderson, Joseph L. and Maud Oakes. *Wisdom of the Serpent.* New York: Collier Books, 1963.

Hume, Lotta Carswell. *Favorite Children's Stories from China and Tibet.* Rutland, Vt.: Charles E. Tuttle Co., 1962.

Husain, Shahrukh. *Demons, Gods, and Holy Men.* New York: Schocken Books, 1987.

Jacobs, Joseph, ed. *Celtic Fairy Tales.* New York: G. P. Putnam's Sons, 1899.

———. *English Fairy Tales.* New York: G. P. Putnam's Sons, 1902.

Jagendorf, M. A. and R. S. Boggs, eds. *The King of the Mountains: A Treasury of Latin American Folk Stories.* New York: Vanguard Press, 1960.

Leland, Charles Godfrey. *Legends of Florence.* New York: Macmillan Company, 1895.

Neugroschel, Joachim, ed. *Yenne Velt: The Great Works of Jewish Fantasy and Occult.* New York: Pocket Books, 1976.

Parrinder, Edward Geoffrey. *African Mythology.* London: Hamlyn Publishing Group, 1967.

Podwal, Mark. *A Book of Hebrew Letters.* Philadelphia: Jewish Publication Society of America, 1978.

Puckett, N. Niles. *Folk Beliefs of the Southern Negro.* Chapel Hill: University of North Carolina Press, 1926.

Radin, Paul and James J. Sweeney, eds. *African Folktales & Sculpture.* Bollingen Series XXXII. New York: Pantheon Books, 1952.

Routledge, W. S. and K. *With a Prehistoric People: The Akikuyu of British East Africa.* London: Edward Arnold, 1910.

de Sahagun, Fray Bernardino. *The Ceremonies.* Part III of *Florentine Codex — Book II.* Translated by Arthur J. O. Anderson and Charles E. Dibble. Santa Fe: School of American Research in association with University of Utah, 1951.

Sakade, Florence, ed. *Japanese Children's Favorite Stories.* Rutland, Vt.: Charles E. Tuttle Co., 1958.

Sampson, John. *Gypsy Folk Tales.* Country Classics. Salem, N.H.: Salem House, 1984.

Scholem, Gershom. *On the Kabbalah and Its Symbolism.* Translated by Ralph Manheim. New York: Schocken Books, 1965.

Spence, Lewis. *North American Myths and Legends: North American Indians.* New York: Avenel Books, 1986; distributed by Crown Publishers.

Stephens, James. *Irish Fairy Tales.* New York: Macmillan Company, 1928.

Vaillant, George C. *Aztecs of Mexico: Origin, Rise, and Fall of the Aztec Nation.* Garden City, N.Y.: Doubleday & Company, 1962.

Warner, Elizabeth. *Heroes, Monsters and Other Worlds from Russian Mythology.* New York: Schocken Books, 1985.

Werner, E. T. C. *Myths and Legends of China.* Singapore: Graham Brash PTE, 1922. Reprint. 1985, 1987.

Wyndam, Lee. *Folk Tales of China.* Indianapolis, Ind.: Bobbs-Merrill, 1963.

Williams-Ellis, Amabel. *Fairy Tales from the British Isles.* 1960. Reprint. New York: Warne, 1964.

Yeats, W. B., ed. *Irish Folk and Fairy Tales.* New York: Boni and Liveright, 1918.

Permission was granted to use source material from:
Grimms' Tales for Young and Old, translated by Ralph Manheim, published by Doubleday;
The Mythology of North America, by John Bierhorst, published by William Morrow & Company;
Ma'aseh Book, translated by Moses Gaster, published by The Jewish Publication Society of America;
Irish Folk and Fairy Tales, edited by William Butler Yeats, published by Random House Inc.;
With a Prehistoric People, by W. S. and K. Routledge, published by Frank Cass & Company Ltd.;
Demons, Gods, and Holy Men, by Shahrukh Husain, published by Eurobook Limited (Peter Lowe);
Myths and Legends of China, by E. T. C. Werner, published by Graham Brash Pte. Ltd.

Permission was also granted to use a quote from Dylan Thomas's
Poems of Dylan Thomas, copyright 1952 by Dylan Thomas.
Reprinted by permission of New Directions Publishing Corporation. U.S. rights;
for Canadian and British rights, refer to: David Higham Associates Ltd.,
5-8 Lower John Street, Golden Square, London WIR 4HA, England.

The paintings in this book were done in acrylics on
D'Arches 140-lb. cold-press watercolor paper.
The display type was set in Athenaeum.
The text type was set in Simoncini Garamond.
Composition by Thompson Type, San Diego, California
Color separations were made by Bright Arts, Ltd., Singapore.
Printed by Holyoke Lithograph, Springfield, Massachusetts
Bound by The Book Press, Brattleboro, Vermont
Production supervision by Warren Wallerstein and Ginger Boyer
Designed by Michael Farmer